# Lucky Me

## Robert Caisley

A SAMUEL FRENCH ACTING EDITION

SAMUEL FRENCH

FOUNDED 1830

SAMUELFRENCH.COM
SAMUELFRENCH-LONDON.CO.UK

## FOR PRODUCTION ENQUIRIES

### UNITED STATES AND CANADA
Info@SamuelFrench.com
1-866-598-8449

### UNITED KINGDOM AND EUROPE
Plays@SamuelFrench-London.co.uk
020-7255-4302

Each title is subject to availability from Samuel French, depending
upon country of performance. Please be aware that *LUCKY ME* may
not be licensed by Samuel French in your territory. Professional and
amateur producers should contact the nearest Samuel French office or
licensing partner to verify availability.

## MUSIC USE NOTE

Licensees are solely responsible for obtaining formal written permission from copyright owners to use copyrighted music in the performance of this play and are strongly cautioned to do so. If no such permission is obtained by the licensee, then the licensee must use only original music that the licensee owns and controls. Licensees are solely responsible and liable for all music clearances and shall indemnify the copyright owners of the play(s) and their licensing agent, Samuel French, against any costs, expenses, losses and liabilities arising from the use of music by licensees. Please contact the appropriate music licensing authority in your territory for the rights to any incidental music.

## IMPORTANT BILLING AND CREDIT REQUIREMENTS

If you have obtained performance rights to this title, please refer to your licensing agreement for important billing and credit requirements.

*LUCKY ME* was first produced in a Rolling World Premiere, as part of the National New Play Network's Continued Life Program at the following theatres:

*LUCKY ME* opened on July 31, 2014 at New Jersey Repertory Company (Gabor Barabas, Executive Producer; SuzAnne Barabas, Artistic Director) in Long Branch, New Jersey. The director was SuzAnne Barabas; the set design and properties were by Jessica Parks; the costume design was by Patricia E. Doherty; the lighting design was by Jill Nagle; the sound design was by Merek Royce Press; the technical director was Michael "Rusty" Carroll; the production stage manager was Jennifer Tardibuono. The cast was as follows:

**SARA FINE**......................................Wendy Peace
**TOM** .......................................Michael Irvin Pollard
**LEO** ...........................................Dan Grimaldi
**YURI** ..........................................Mark Light-Orr

*LUCKY ME* opened on October 24, 2014 at Curious Theatre (Chip Walton, Producing Artistic Director) in Denver, Colorado. The director was Chip Walton; the set design was by Markas Henry; the costume design was by Kevin Brainerd; the lighting design was by Jacob Welch; the sound design was by Brian Freeland; with properties by Kristin Hamer; the technical director was Mark Wethington; the production stage manager was Rachel Ducat. The cast was as follows:

**SARA FINE**.....................................Dee Covington
**TOM** ..........................................Erik Sandvold
**LEO** ...........................................Randy Moore
**YURI** ..........................................Kurt Brighton

*LUCKY ME* opened on January 30, 2015 at Riverside Theatre (Jody Hovland, Artistic Director; Jennifer Holan, Executive Director) in Iowa City, Iowa. The director was Jody Hovland; the scenic design and properties were by Shelly A. Ford; the costume design was by Osean Perez; the lighting design and sound design were by Drew Bielinski; the technical director was Violet Virnig; the production stage manager was Rachel Potthoff. The cast was as follows:

**SARA FINE**....................................Jennifer Fawcett
**TOM** .........................................Patrick DuLaney
**LEO** .............................................Ron Clark
**YURI** ............................................Tim Budd

*LUCKY ME* opened on April 10, 2015 at Oregon Contemporary Theatre (Craig Willis, Producing Artistic Director) in Eugene, Oregon. The director was Patrick Torelle; the set design was by Jeffrey Cook; the costume design was by Erin Schindler; the lighting design was by Amanda Baca; the sound design was by Gabe Carlin; with special effects by Amy Dunn, and properties by Andrew Frederick; the production stage manager was Bryanna Rainwater. The cast was as follows:

| | |
|---|---|
| **SARA FINE** | Kelly Quinnett |
| **TOM** | Eric Hadley |
| **LEO** | Joe Cronin |
| **YURI** | Tony Stirpe |

## CHARACTERS

**SARA FINE** – in her 40s
**TOM** – her neighbor, around the same age; he works for the TSA
**LEO** – Sara's elderly father; he is blind
**YURI** – the landlord, whatever age works; he is Ukrainian

## SETTING

Denver, Colorado.
Sara's second-floor, two bedroom apartment.

## TIME

Between New Year's Eve and July 4th of the same year.

## ACKNOWLEDGEMENTS

The playwright wishes to thank the following individuals and organizations for their assistance and generous support during the writing and development of this play: SuzAnne and Gabor Barabas, Jere Hodgin, Greg Johnson and the Missoula Writers Colony, Nan Barnett and the National New Play Network. With very special thanks to the Idaho Commission on the Arts and the National Endowment for the Arts.

## AUTHOR'S NOTES

The script contains some "special effects" which overall contribute to the great fun, but also the great challenge of producing this play. I have seen these technical issues solved in a variety of ways, but I have found that the very simplest solutions have proved to be the most effective, both visually and cost-wise. Some of the effects are rudimentary, while others a little more elaborate, but it is the combined effect of all this "weirdness" – as it's described in the play – that lends LUCKY ME its whimsical appeal as a very different kind of comedy. None of the effects are beyond the capabilities of any theatre, regardless of size or budget. I do, however, encourage directors and producers to begin thinking about these technical challenges as early in the process as possible, and think of them almost like another character in the play. I offer some thoughts on production at the end of the script.

*This play is dedicated to Jean Bruce Scott.*

# ACT ONE

## One

*(It is 2:30 in the morning on New Year's Day. The stage is dark and empty. From the hallway outside, we hear muffled voices, someone coming noisily up the stairs.)*

**SARA.** *(off)* This is me.

**TOM.** *(off)* Where's the switch?

**SARA.** *(off)* The light's burnt out.

**TOM.** *(off)* Where's the key?

**SARA.** *(off)* My back pocket, can you grab it?

**TOM.** *(off)* Sure, hold on.

*(A jingle of keys. The door swings open.)*

There we go. Mission accomplished.

*(In the low light now streaming in we can barely make out TOM, helping a woman on crutches, her foot in an orthopedic boot, into the apartment. This is SARA FINE. She wears a coat over pajamas. TOM is dressed for arctic weather.)*

**SARA.** I really gotta pee!

**TOM.** Let me get the lights.

**SARA.** Don't go anywhere.

**TOM.** You need any help?

**SARA.** Peeing?

**TOM.** With your foot.

**SARA.** I don't use my feet to pee.

**TOM.** No, I just meant…

**SARA.** Kidding. Make yourself at home.

(**SARA** *hobbles off in the direction of the bathroom.* **TOM** *looks around the dark apartment. He hits the nearest light switch. Nothing happens.*)

**TOM.** Hey.

You got a bulb out.

(**TOM** *goes to another light switch. Nada.*)

You got two bulbs out.

**SARA.** *(off)* Thanks.

**TOM.** Plus the one on the staircase…which is a major safety issue.

(*He tries one more switch.*)

I think maybe the power's out.

All the snow and ice? Maybe took out a power line.

**SARA.** *(off)* Yeah, no.

**TOM.** Or you've blown a fuse. Where's the fuse box?

**SARA.** *(off)* No, I just have a problem with bulbs.

They burn out.

**TOM.** You should try those new kind, you know, the curly things? Incandescent deals?

**SARA.** *(off)* Fluorescent.

**TOM.** Huh?

**SARA.** *(off)* You said incandescent. You meant fluorescent.

**TOM.** Yeah, the curly things. They last forever.

**SARA.** *(off)* No, they burn out too.

**TOM.** You got any candles?

Maybe a flashlight?

I got flashlights up the wazoo but God knows which box I packed 'em in.

(*beat*)

**SARA.** *(off)* Did you just say "up the wazoo?"

**TOM.** Yeah.

**SARA.** *(off)* Okay.

    *(beat)*

    I got bulbs.

    I keep extras.

**TOM.** Good for you.

    Emergency preparedness.

    You never know, right?

    *(a beat)*

    Where am I lookin?

**SARA.** *(off)* In the kitchen. The cupboard. With the calendar.

    (**TOM** *notices her calendar: it has cats on it.*)

**TOM.** Cute calendar. Do you have a cat?

**SARA.** *(off)* Sometimes.

    (**TOM** *looks in her direction.*)

    (*He opens the cupboard.*)

    (*It contains nothing but light bulbs.*)

**TOM.** Wow! That's a lot of bright ideas! Does this happen a lot?

**SARA.** *(off)* Huh?

**TOM.** The bulb thing?

**SARA.** *(off)* Yeah, I told you I gotta problem with bulbs.

    (**TOM** *relocates a chair to help him replace one of the burnt out bulbs; he starts taking it out of its package.*)

**TOM.** *(like it's an interesting story, except it's not)* Maybe I'm exaggerating to make a point, but seriously. I think I've changed like ten light bulbs my whole life. I don't think I'm making that up. It's so rare, it's such a surprise when one burns out, I'm like…*that's weird.*

**SARA.** *(off)* You're lucky.

    Mine don't last that long.

    (*We hear a toilet flushing.*)

**TOM.** How long do yours last?

(**TOM** *screws in the first bulb and the light pops on just as* **SARA** *comes back in, minus the coat.*)

**SARA.** I spent forty-seven hundred bucks on bulbs last year.

(**TOM** *stares at her. Did he hear her right?*)

You want something to drink?

(**TOM** *nods, 'Yes,' removes his parka and continues to replace the other two burnt out bulbs in the living room.*)

**TOM.** There's gotta be some kind of electrical surge. You should probably have the landlord check it out.

**SARA.** He checked it out last week.

**TOM.** And?

**SARA.** He slipped on the ice; he's in a neck brace, so… I didn't want to bug him. Orange juice okay?

(*He gives her a 'thumbs up.'*)

Actually, do you mind getting it yourself? I really need to sit down.

(*She hobbles to the couch and collapses onto it with a sigh of relief.*)

**TOM.** (*Heading for kitchen area*) I'd take a look myself, but I'm not really one of those D.I.Y. guys, you know?

**SARA.** You look really self-sufficient.

**TOM.** Yeah, no. Shoveling snow and changing bulbs is about the extent of my home improvement skills. It's funny: I asked you where your fuse box was.

**SARA.** Why's that funny?

**TOM.** Because I'm not entirely sure what you do with a fuse box once you find it.

**SARA.** (*Duh!*) Check the breaker?

**TOM.** See: all these technical terms.

(**TOM** *grabs the O.J. from the fridge.*)

Fridge light's out.

**SARA.** Drawer to the right.

*(He finds and holds up a small bulb for her to see, right above his head.)*

**TOM.** Bing! Get it?

**SARA.** Uhuh.

*(We get the feeling she's heard this a million times before.* **TOM** *replaces the fridge bulb.)*

**TOM.** Hey, sorry about the thing. Earlier. In the hallway. On the stairs?

**SARA.** What thing?

**TOM.** When I grabbed your key?

**SARA.** Oh.

**TOM.** From your back pocket?
    And I kinda – ?

**SARA.** Groped me?

**TOM.** Yeah.
    I normally don't do that.

**SARA.** That's good.

**TOM.** I mean: I normally don't get that close to people.

**SARA.** Okay.

**TOM.** On a regular basis, I'm sayin'.
    Where I…you know, because of…
    *Proximity* an' all, I…accidentally –

**SARA.** Grope them?

**TOM.** Right.

**SARA.** I thought you worked at the airport.

**TOM.** I do work at the airport.

**SARA.** For TSA.

**TOM.** Yeah.

**SARA.** I would think accidentally groping people was a –

**TOM.** 'Occupational hazard?'

**SARA.** I was gonna say 'resume builder.'

**TOM.** Yeah, well, I was referring to…non work-related groping. So…sorry.

SARA. It's the least I could do. I didn't get a chance to thank
   you at the hospital.

TOM. Forget it.

SARA. No, really. Who wants to spend New Year's Eve in the
   emergency room – ?

TOM. Hey, free coffee.

SARA. – With a total stranger?

TOM. It was a nice distraction from all those boxes I gotta
   unpack.

SARA. You don't like hospitals do you? You seemed real
   agitated.

TOM. *(He looks agitated, then…)* – And what was I doing
   interrogating the doctor with all those lame questions?

SARA. Right?

TOM. – Like I had *any* clue what he was saying? I'm just a
   weirdo tonight.

   *(He hands her a glass of O.J.)*

   O.J. for the little lady. *(catches himself)* See, that's not a
   cool joke.

SARA. Well, thanks, weirdo. For coming to my rescue. And
   welcome to the neighborhood, I guess.

TOM. Cheers!

   *(***TOM*** clinks glasses with **SARA** and **SARA**'s shatters,
   spilling juice all over her. She doesn't react at all.)*

   Oh, shit, I'm sorry!

   *(Horrified, **TOM** runs to the kitchen and grabs a roll of
   paper towels.)*

SARA. It happens all the time, don't worry about it.

   *(He laughs.)*

   What's funny?

TOM. "It happens all the time."

SARA. Yeah?

TOM. It happens all the time?
   Your glasses shatter all the time?

**SARA.** I don't usually use *these* except for company, which I rarely have. I got plastic for everyday use. You weren't to know.

*(He stares at her. He goes back to the kitchen, pours her some more juice in a plastic cup and grabs a wet cloth.)*

**TOM.** Sorry about the couch.

**SARA.** That's what the plastic's for.

*(And it's now, that **TOM** realizes all the furniture in the apartment is covered in plastic.)*

Hey: was I a bitch? I was bitchy, wasn't I? At the hospital. You can tell me.

**TOM.** *(diplomatically)* You were in pain.

**SARA.** So that's a 'yes.'

**TOM.** *(re: her foot)* How's it feeling by the way? Now the drugs kicked in.

**SARA.** My armpits hurt.

The foot's fine, actually, the pits are kinda raw.

**TOM.** You got a sweat sock?

**SARA.** *(dubious)* Why…?

**TOM.** *(pointing off)* You mind?

**SARA.** It's a mess back there. Go like that:

*(She makes a gesture like she's wearing blinders. **TOM** follows suit and walks off toward the bedrooms.)*

**TOM.** *(off)* Hey, I like that thing above your bed. What is it?

**SARA.** You're not supposed to be looking. *(Duh!)* It's called a photo?

**TOM.** *(off)* Awesome. Is that you as a kid?

**SARA.** Uhuh.

**TOM.** *(off)* With your dad?

**SARA.** Uhuh.

**TOM.** *(off)* Is he still with us?

**SARA.** Last time I checked.

**TOM.** *(off)* You got another bulb out in the hallway, F.Y.I. *And* the guest room.

**SARA.** That's dad's room.

  What are you doing anyway?

  *(He returns with two rolled-up athletic socks, which he unfurls.)*

**TOM.** Little padding's all you need.

  **(TOM** *wraps the socks around the head of each of her crutches as the following dialogue continues.)*

**SARA.** Thought you weren't much of a handy-man?

**TOM.** Live and learn. I broke the same little bone two summers ago.

**SARA.** Get outta here.

**TOM.** Same exact spot.

  I guess we're twinsies.

  *(He hands her the crutches. She tries it.)*

**SARA.** *(re: the crutch)* Oh, that's so much better.

  So what *you* do to get your very own "Dancer's Fracture"?

**TOM.** Well:

  …I wasn't up on any roof, I can tell ya that.

  *(She just stares at him.)*

  Cleaning the gutters?

  In your bathrobe?

  In an ice storm?

  On New Year's Eve…?

  *(beat)*

  What were you doing up there – ?

**SARA.** – I should probably let you get back to your unpacking.

**TOM.** *(an attempt at humor)* You can tell me. I can take it.

  *(She looks at him. Should she tell him?)*

**SARA.** There's a leak. That's been driving me crazy. Seriously. Whenever it rains: drip, drip, drip. Like the Chinese water torture. *And* it's going right into my fish tank, *and* it's screwing up the ph or whatever *and* it's probably gonna kill my fish, so…

(**TOM** *drifts over to the fish tank. He looks at the fish. He looks up at the ceiling.*)

**TOM.** Why don't you move the fish tank?

**SARA.** I have.

(*And it's now that* **TOM** *realizes there are leaks in several spots from the ceiling, and several buckets throughout the living room to catch the drips.*)

**TOM.** Wow!

(*assessing it like a pro*) I guess what you got here…is a bit of a leaky roof.

(*Beat. He checks out the fish.*)

What're your fish called?

**SARA.** Fish.

(*He looks at her.*)

**TOM.** Both of 'em?

**SARA.** I try not to get attached.

(*beat*)

Hey, so: what's your excuse?

(*She points at her injured foot.*)

Twinsies?

**TOM.** Oh. Right. I was, in fact, dancing.

**SARA.** Dancing?

**TOM.** In fact, I was.

**SARA.** You got a Dancer's Fracture from *actual* dancing?

**TOM.** I have some moves, yeah.

**SARA.** What kind of dancing?

**TOM.** Salsa.

**SARA.** Get outta here!

**TOM.** I will not.

**SARA.** You were Salsa dancing –

**TOM.** With my ex.

**SARA**. – and you made one of your moves –

**TOM**. One of my *signature* moves.

**SARA**. – and *actually* sustained a fracture of the fifth metatarsal.

**TOM**. Yeah, but I told people I was mountain biking.

**SARA**. Okay.

**TOM**. And went off a cliff. 'Cause it sounds…

**SARA**. Got it.

**TOM**. Much more… *grrrrrr*

*(He makes a weird hand gesture like he's gunning downhill on a mountain bike.)*

**SARA**. Right.

**TOM**. …much less… *(another gesture; a flourish)* Olé, y'know?

*(SARA nods.)*

*(pause)*

**SARA**. Why'd you tell me?

**TOM**. Huh?

**SARA**. About the dancing? The signature move?
If it's so…embarrassing? Why'd you come clean?

**TOM**. Yeah, I dunno.

*(He thinks about it: he still doesn't know.)*

Now I'm naked before you. I guess.

*(They stare at each other awkwardly.)*

*(pause)*

You live with your dad?

**SARA**. He lives with me.

**TOM**. Awesome.

*(SARA's not sure about that.)*

I'd love to meet him.

**SARA**. Why?

**TOM**. When he's home next?

**SARA**. He never goes anywhere.

He's back there right now.

(**TOM** *looks down the hallway.*)

**TOM.** In the dark?

**SARA.** You don't wanna meet him…why'd you want to meet him?

**TOM.** Err… you know.

(*He doesn't know.*)

Just being neighborly.

**SARA.** Dad doesn't really *do* neighbors.

**TOM.** How come?

(**LEO FINE, SARA**'s *elderly father appears from the hallway. He's dressed smartly in a suit. He's carrying a briefcase like he's on his way out the door to go to work. He is blind. [Does he have a cane? If he does, he only uses it occasionally, having a pretty good sense of the layout of the place. Regardless, it's essential that we understand right away he's blind.]*)

**LEO.** Who the hell are you?

(**TOM** *startles.*)

**TOM.** Jesus!!! I didn't see you back there.

**LEO.** I didn't see you either.

**SARA.** Hi dad.

**TOM.** I'm sorry.

**LEO.** Are you sellin' something?

**SARA.** This is Tom.

**LEO.** What's he sellin'?

**SARA.** This is Leo.

**TOM.** Hi, no. No, I'm –

**SARA.** He's a friend of mine.

**LEO.** I don't know about that.

**SARA.** We just met, actually.

**TOM.** She fell off the roof.

**LEO.** Who did?

**TOM.** Your daughter?

**LEO.** Which one?

**SARA.** You only have one, Dad.

**LEO.** That sounds about right.

**SARA.** Sara.

**LEO.** Sara was on the roof?

**SARA.** I broke a bone in my foot. Tom helped me.

**LEO.** You're a doctor?

**TOM.** I'm in security.

**LEO.** What's a security guard doing giving out medical advice?

**TOM.** No, *Homeland* Security.

**SARA.** No, Dad, he found me.

**LEO.** Huh?

**TOM.** After she fell.

**SARA.** I fell off the roof and Tom found me.
    He just moved in across the street.

**LEO.** *My* street?

**SARA.** It's not your street Dad.

**LEO.** We'll see about that.

**TOM.** Yeah, I'm err, right over… well, actually… you can see it from here.

    *(He moves toward the window, pointing.)*

    The white building? With the little…err…

    *(He realizes his mistake; stands dumbly at the window. Beat.)*

**LEO.** You fell off the roof?

**SARA.** Yeah.

**LEO.** That was pretty stupid.
    And you broke your ankle?

**SARA.** Just one little bone.

**LEO.** And you work security?

**TOM.** At the airport.

**LEO.** You're one of them creeps likes to feel everybody up.

**TOM.** Apparently.

**LEO.** Why aren't you at the airport?

**TOM.** Haven't started yet. Just transferred in.

**LEO.** From where?

**TOM.** Juneau.

**LEO.** They got an airport there?

**TOM.** A little one, yeah.

**LEO.** Why'd you come here?

**TOM.** They got a bigger one.

**LEO.** *(to* **SARA***)* Does that sound safe to you?
Is this guy even qualified?

**SARA.** Daddy!

**LEO.** What kinda threat-level they got up in Juneau?
Do terrorists even go that far north?

**TOM.** Yes, sir, I think so, sir.

**LEO.** Why? Is it for the fishing?

**TOM.** Well, no there's the, uh, whaddayacallem…strategic oil reserves.

**LEO.** Oil?

**TOM.** Uhuh.

**LEO.** In Alaska.

**TOM.** We got oil up the wazoo.

(**SARA** *laughs.*)

**LEO.** What do they want *my* oil for? They got their own, don't they?

**TOM.** Sir?

**LEO.** The terrorists? Don't they have enough of their own?

**TOM.** I don't know, I guess.

**LEO.** Well, do they or don't they?

**TOM.** That's not exactly my area of expertise.

**LEO.** You're the first line of defense, aren't ya?
Shouldn't it be? Shouldn't these larger philosophical questions *be* your "area of expertise?"

**TOM.** I'm just a screener. I screen luggage. I screen passengers.

**LEO.** You *grope* passengers.

**TOM.** No, I –

**LEO.** You deprive them of moisturizer.

**SARA.** Okay, Dad.

**LEO.** What exactly are you looking for?

**TOM.** Err…

**LEO.** The tell-tale signs? Do you *know* the tell-tale signs? D'you receive *any* special training before they sent you down here to my airport?

**SARA.** It's not your airport, Daddy.

**LEO.** Because if you didn't, that's the last time I fly out of that death trap.

**SARA.** *(sotto voce to* **TOM***)* He hasn't been on a plane in twenty years.

*(Pause.* **LEO** *is not satisfied with any of this guy's answers.)*

**LEO.** What were you doin' on my roof, anyway?

**SARA.** It's my roof, Dad.

**LEO.** What were you doin' on her roof?

**TOM.** I wasn't on the roof.

**SARA.** He was a bystander.

**LEO.** That's what they all say!

**TOM.** Sara was on the roof, sir.

**LEO.** *(to* **SARA***, shaking his head disapprovingly)* Boy! Where'd you land this time?

**TOM.** She um – it's funny – she's lucky the hedge broke her fall, or it'd be more than her fifth metatarsal busted.

**LEO.** Meta-what?

**TOM.** It's the little bone between…
    This time???
    You said, where'd you land *this* time?
    *(to* **SARA***)* You've fallen off the roof before?

**SARA**. *(oddly, in her own defense)* Well, not this roof.

**TOM**. You've fallen off *a* roof before?

**LEO**. Oh, she's always falling off roofs.

**SARA**. Okay, dad.

**LEO**. She falls off all kinds of things.

**SARA**. Let's get you to bed.

**LEO**. I just woke up.

**SARA**. It's almost three a.m.

**LEO**. That doesn't sound right. Is she lying to me?

**TOM**. No, sir, it'll be daylight soon.

**LEO**. What do I care?

**TOM**. Be careful, it's dark back there.

**LEO**. Okay, funny man!

**TOM**. No, I was just –

**LEO**. *(suddenly irate)* Mind your own damn business! This is America: a man can be in the dark if he wants!

**TOM**. *(an appeal to* **SARA***)* I could replace the bulbs if you want.

**LEO**. What's the point? They'll just burn right out. They don't make 'em like they used to. In my day? Boy, they used to really know how to make a light bulb. What do they expect: outsourcing all those American jobs to twelve year olds in Mumbai. What does a twelve-year-old know about light bulbs?

**TOM**. I was telling Sara that I think you've maybe got some kind of electrical problem.

**LEO**. Are you an electrician now, or somethin'?

**TOM**. No, I –

(**SARA** *is struggling to corral her father, but it's tricky with crutches.*)

**SARA**. Come on, dad.

**LEO**. I gotta get to the office.

**SARA**. The office is closed, Dad.

**LEO**. There's people out there who need protection!

**SARA.** You can take care of it in the morning, Dad.

**LEO.** *(agitated)* Don't let me forget!

**SARA.** I won't.

**LEO.** All it takes is a moment's inattention!

(**SARA** *is ushering* **LEO** *out.*)

**TOM.** It was nice to meet you, sir.

**LEO.** *(to* **SARA***)* I wish he'd stop with the "sir" business.

**SARA.** Let's hit the hay.

**LEO.** Did I miss the fireworks?

I missed the fireworks again, goddamn it!

*(to* **SARA***)* D'you watch 'em with that TSA fella?

**SARA.** He took me to the hospital.

**LEO.** What kind of a date is that?

**TOM.** It wasn't a date. It was an emergency.

**LEO.** That's what they all say.

**TOM.** Good night, Leo.

**LEO.** *(to* **SARA***)* Who is he again?

**SARA.** Thanks again, Tom.

**TOM.** I'll see myself out.

(**SARA** *and* **LEO** *start to exit.*)

Sara? Happy New Year.

(**SARA** *smiles, then heads off. We hear music: "Auld Lang Syne."*)

(*Before leaving,* **TOM** *takes a light bulb from the cupboard, opens the front door and sets his sights on the hallway light fixture. He looks briefly back inside then shuts the door behind him.*)

(*As he does, one of the new bulbs that* **TOM** *replaced earlier flickers and goes out.*)

## Two

*(A couple weeks later. LEO is in the kitchen area fixing himself a sandwich. His briefcase is on the counter. Once again, he is dressed smartly in suit and tie. SARA is at the fish tank with a little net. She's scooping a dead fish out of the tank and into a little container. LEO grabs a bottle of mustard from the refrigerator and holds it up.)*

LEO. Is this the kind I like?

SARA. Uhuh.

LEO. We're gettin' low.

SARA. I'll get more.

LEO. Bread, too.

SARA. Okay.

LEO. It's suspiciously stiff.

SARA. Okay, dad.

LEO. You want one?

SARA. I'm not hungry.

LEO. You should eat.
You know what they say? "Feed a cold"…something else a fever.

SARA. Oh, is that what they say?

LEO. Last time I checked.

*(LEO makes a big deal of squeezing the remaining mustard noisily from the bottle.)*

SARA. "Starve."

LEO. Huh?

SARA. "Starve a fever."

LEO. Well, there you go. You got a fever?

SARA. No.

LEO. Then what further evidence do you need? I'll make you a little sandwich. With the crusts cut off. The way you like it.

SARA. I like crusts.

**LEO.** That musta been your sister.

    (**SARA** *sighs.*)

**SARA.** I don't have a cold, dad. Or a fever. Or a sister.
I broke a little bone in my foot. We've been over this.
I don't think eating or not eating's gonna make a
difference.

**LEO.** You broke your foot?

**SARA.** We've been over –

**LEO.** *(impressed with himself)* The 5th meta-tarsal!

    (*They're both a little impressed.*)

**SARA.** You remembered.

**LEO.** Of course I remembered. *(taps his forehead)* My brain's
a steel trap. *(He sits to eat his sandwich.)* Your mother
would tell me, all week long, whatever she needed
at the store. Monday through Friday, she'd blurt out
item after item, and I'd say, "Sure, Gracie," and she'd
say, "Leo, write it down," and I'd say, "Gracie, don't
you worry about it, it's all up here." *(He taps his steel
trap.)* And sure enough: Saturday morning I'd go
to the store, I'd go to *five different* stores, and *bango!*
Instant recall. I never once forgot a single item, a
single necessity that woman wanted, all the years of
our marriage.

    (*He takes a bite of his sandwich.*)

**SARA.** Estelle, dad.
Gracie was your sister.

    (*He stops chewing, considering the implications of this.*)

**LEO.** The point still stands.

    (*He chews a few more chews.*)

This cheese is questionable.
How old is this cheese?

**SARA.** I got it last week.

**LEO.** No, there's something iffy about this cheese.
It's pungent.

**SARA.** Cheese is supposed to be pungent.

**LEO.** Not this kind.

This is good old-fashioned American cheese.

It's supposed to have a decided *lack* of pungency.

**SARA.** Fine, I'll get more.

**LEO.** This is makin' my eyes water.

**SARA.** Then don't eat it, I'll get more.

(**LEO** *chews his sandwich, looking over in his daughter's direction.*)

**LEO.** Do you know when, exactly?

**SARA.** I'm a little busy right now.

(*pause*)

**LEO.** You hear about it all the time.

Food-borne illnesses.

People lose their lives.

Many people.

Many innocent people.

Many innocent *elderly* people.

**SARA.** Jesus, Dad, you're not gonna die from eating some week-old funky cheese. I'll get some when I get some. I'm not exactly *functional* right now. So make a list.

**LEO.** I don't need a list.

(*He taps his steel trap.*)

**SARA.** Make one anyway. For us mortals!

**LEO.** I'll type one up at the office.

After I finish this questionable cheese sandwich.

**SARA.** Look, if you don't want it, toss it out.

**LEO.** Are you nuts? Who knows when you'll be fit enough to replenish the stores. We better conserve.

**SARA.** Fine.

D'you take your pills?

**LEO.** Already took 'em.

(**SARA** *is doubtful.*)

**SARA.** Two in the morning, two at night.

> *(This is a thing they do.)*

**LEO.** Two in the morning, two at night.

> *(***SARA*** *continues work on the fish tank.* **LEO** *pulls out a Ziploc bag and packs up the rest of his sandwich. He puts it in his briefcase and starts to put on his overcoat. He hears the sloshing of tank water.)*

**LEO.** What are you up to, anyhow?

**SARA.** The fish died again.

**LEO.** We had fish?

> I thought we had a cat.

**SARA.** Me too.

**LEO.** *(somewhat philosophically)* I like the idea of having fish. Sounds calming.

> Did you ever just sit and watch 'em swimming around? Little weightless colorful things?

**SARA.** I did.

**LEO.** That sounds nice.

> What happened? The cat get 'em?

**SARA.** That was last time.

**LEO.** That's right. This time?

**SARA.** The water got contaminated.

**LEO.** We should look into that.

> The water supply is critical. Read your history books.

> *(She nods.)*

> What happened to the cat?

**SARA.** You got me.

**LEO.** Did he leave a note or anything?

> *(***SARA*** *smiles.)*

> Was it that ugly fat thing would sit on my lap, make my legs go numb?

**SARA.** He got hit by a car. Don't you remember?

**LEO.** One summer.

**SARA.** Last summer.

**LEO.** That dippy teenager.

**SARA.** He was sweet.

**LEO.** He was dippy. If I recall.

**SARA.** He didn't have to knock on every door. I thought that was really sweet. You were mean to him.

**LEO.** I was trying to instill a sense of personal responsibility.

**SARA.** You flushed his car keys down the toilet.

**LEO.** I can't be expected to be courteous to every Tom, Dick and Harry that knocks at my door.

**SARA.** Well, it's not your door.

**LEO.** It used to be my door.

**SARA.** It was never your door.

**LEO.** *(suddenly irate)* Listen, young lady –

**SARA.** Okay, dad –

**LEO.** – I used to have a door that looked very much like that door! I used to have *lots* of doors. You understand? There was a time –

**SARA.** I'm sorry, dad.

**LEO.** There was a time...

**SARA.** I said I'm sorry.

*(pause)*

**LEO.** Well, I can't stand around blathering with you. I gotta meeting downtown.

*(He heads for the door but stops short, listening to the sound of the water sloshing in the tank.)*

What's the death toll this time?

**SARA.** Two.

**LEO.** *(He suddenly remembers.)* Last time was six. Quite a massacre. If I recall.
You only had two?

**SARA.** These guys were expensive.

*(A beat. LEO removes his overcoat.)*

LEO. You know, maybe I won't go to the office today. Maybe I'll stay home, play hooky with my little girl.

SARA. That'd be nice.

LEO. Don't tell your mother.

(*He shuffles over to* SARA *with his briefcase.*)

Should we say something?

SARA. Okay.

LEO. A few words. To commemorate their life.

SARA. That'd be nice.

(*They stand together by the empty tank.*)

LEO. Dear Heavenly Father:

(*He clears his throat.*)

(*He shifts uneasily on his feet.*)

(*He clears his throat again.*)

SARA. Dad...?

LEO. (*suddenly overcome with emotion*) You know, I don't think I can.

SARA. It's okay.

LEO. I'm sorry, honey. Maybe I could...

(*He points off down the hallway.*)

SARA. That's fine, dad, go ahead.

LEO. I'll call you.

(*LEO shuffles out of the room.* SARA *watches him exit. She struggles over to the couch with one crutch and collapses with relief. And just as she gets settled...*)

(*There is a very soft knock at the door.* SARA *freezes, unaccustomed to people knocking on her door.*)

SARA. Yeah...?

TOM. (*off*) Sara?

SARA. Yes?

TOM. (*off*) It's Tom?

**SARA.** Yeah?

**TOM.** *(off)* From across the street?

**SARA.** Yeah?

**TOM.** *(off)* You okay?

**SARA.** Yeah.

**TOM.** *(off)* Can I come in?

**SARA.** Yeah.

> *(The door slowly opens.* **TOM** *enters. He is dressed in his TSA uniform. He's got a fast food bag in one hand, and a pair of saucepans in the other. He looks at the bulb just outside the door that's burnt out again.)*

**TOM.** I thought I fixed that.

Hi.

I was at work.

**SARA.** Okay.

**TOM.** I just got off.

**SARA.** Okay.

**TOM.** *(re: the saucepans)* I found these in the bushes. Out front. Are they yours?

> *(***SARA** *shakes her head, "No.")*

You want 'em?

> *(***SARA** *nods, "Yes."* **TOM** *puts them in the kitchen. He stands, looking at her for a moment.)*

I was five hours into my shift, when this little kid with one of those monkey backpacks goes ape shit 'cause her mom put monkey in the metal detector. And that's when it hit me: how's Sara gonna manage? On crutches? Cooking, or…cleaning, or…whatever?

**SARA.** You just thought of this?

**TOM.** Uhuh.

**SARA.** Two weeks later?

**TOM.** I thought of it the same day, but…it took me a while to…

*(He makes an odd gesture with his hands which apparently explains whatever he was trying to explain.)*

…you know?

*(SARA nods vaguely. Beat.)*

Hope you're not vegetarian.

*(He holds up the bag of food he brought.)*

*(The phone rings. SARA struggles to answer it.)*

*(Johnny-on-the-spot)* Relax, I'll get it.

SARA. No, no, it's my –

TOM. *(into phone)* Hello? This is Tom. Who's this?

*(Maybe we can hear LEO through the phone: he doesn't sound pleased.)*

*(covering the mouthpiece)* I think it's your dad

*(He hands it over. During SARA's call, TOM takes note of the dead fish.)*

SARA. *(into phone)* Hi, dad.
Tom?
From the hospital?
No, from the airport.
No… Tom!
Just checking up on us.

*(She looks over at TOM, then covers the mouthpiece and mutters something incomprehensible.)*

*(to TOM: lying)* He says, 'Hi.'

*(TOM gives a 'thumbs up.')*

*(into the phone)* Yeah, go ahead. I'm ready.

*(She listens to her father speak.)*

*(She listens some more; she is moved; she nods, smiles.)*

Thanks, daddy. That was nice. Yeah. I think they will.
No, you go ahead, I'll be okay.

*(She hangs up.)*

**TOM**. Everything okay?

Does he need a ride home or something? I got the truck in front.

**SARA**. No. He's home.

(**TOM** *looks down the hallway; he looks back at* **SARA***, confused.*)

He calls me.

Sometimes.

If he has something to say...and he can't quite...you know.

Say it.

(**TOM** *nods. He holds up the bag of fast food in acknowledgement, as the lights snap to black.*)

### Three

*(A few days later.* **LEO** *is sitting on the couch with a small typing table before him, on which stands a manual typewriter. He is slowly and meticulously typing something out.* **TOM** *is standing in the doorway, not entirely certain if he should come inside. We sense he's been standing there for a whole. He is holding a plastic bag with a goldfish swimming in it. Mid-story:)*

**TOM**. There was this other guy, right? With his wife. And two kids. And they're about to go through the check point. This was late 2001/2002, so we're still on heightened alert, you know, the *nation*. And we got this K9 unit assigned to us, this pair of beagles specially trained to sniff out a whole range of crap you shouldn't be taking on board a plane: everything from C4 to drugs to…well, contraband, right? And, well: the mom goes through with the little boy, and the dad goes through with the little girl. And the beagles go ballistic. Somethin's triggered their…their whatchamacallit… and all hell breaks loose. TSA uniforms are everywhere, six and seven deep, and the airport police respond, guns drawn. Passengers are freaking out. And these kids, these two kids? *(suppressing his own laughter)* Their backpacks are *stuffed* with pounds and pounds of jerky. Beef jerky, turkey jerky, salmon. They'd been to visit grandma and grandpa, and grandpa had just got himself a dehydrator and fancied himself a jerky connoisseur…

*(***TOM*** smiles, nods.)*

So: that was funny.

*(Silence.* **LEO** *keeps typing.)*

And then this other time? I'm "wanding" this older lady and her crotch starts beeping –

**LEO**. I'm not listening to a word you're saying, you know that, right?

**TOM.** Is Sara home?

**LEO.** What's your name again? Brad?

**TOM.** Tom.

**LEO.** TSA Tom.

**TOM.** Yeah, is she home?

**LEO.** She's probably on the roof.

> (**TOM** *looks skyward.*)

**TOM.** Why would she do that again?

**LEO.** Women are complicated.

How old are you, Tom?

**TOM.** 42.

**LEO.** And you haven't learned that yet?

**TOM.** How would she even get up there?

**LEO.** Wouldn't *you* like to know?

**TOM.** I mean with her *foot* and everything?

**LEO.** Life is full of mysteries, Brad.

**TOM.** Tom.

**LEO.** I once saw a man with two broken legs carry his fallen comrade across a battlefield.

**TOM.** Wow! I didn't know you were in the service.

**LEO.** *(Isn't it obvious?)* I saw it in a movie!

I haven't always been blind, you know.

This is a *recent* development.

**TOM.** Really?

**LEO.** You callin' me a liar?

**TOM.** No, I…

How'd you lose it? Your eyesight.

**LEO.** The usual way.

> (**TOM** *doesn't get it.*)

I just woke up one morning…

**TOM.** *(OMG)* And it was *gone?*

**LEO.** No, I woke up one morning, as usual, and went to the office, as usual, came home, as usual, and this went on for several years, and then I went in for a regular checkup with the eye doctor, as usual, and he said, "Leo, I've got some good news and some bad news. The bad news is you'll lose sight in both your eyes within six months. And you'll never get it back." And, boy, was he right. Six months, to the day. Boom! Lights out!

*(beat)*

**TOM.** What was the good news?

**LEO.** I didn't have to renew my prescription.

(**TOM** *nods, slowly.*)

**TOM.** Maybe I should come back later. You look kinda busy.

**LEO.** I *am* kinda busy.

(**LEO** *lazily punches two or three typewriter keys.*)

**TOM.** What are you doing, exactly? If you don't mind me asking?

**LEO.** Are *you* blind? I'm typing.

What are *you* doing?

I mean that's the more interesting question, don't you think?

Brad?

**TOM.** Tom.

**LEO.** What exactly are *you* doing?

**TOM.** I, I brought Sara something.

And I wanted to drop it off.

It's just a little…

**LEO.** What?

**TOM.** A gift.

**LEO.** A gift?

**TOM.** Uhuh.

**LEO.** You bought her a gift?

**TOM.** Kind of.

**LEO.** You kind of bought my daughter a gift?

**TOM**. Is that okay?

**LEO**. What kind of gift you bring her?

**TOM**. A fish.

**LEO**. Why the hell d'you bring her a fish?

**TOM**. Well, I thought, you know: in light of recent tragic events.

**LEO**. Are you nuts? She's *allergic!*

How long you been married to her?

**TOM**. What? I'm not –

**LEO**. You can't remember these critical details?

**TOM**. I'm not married to Sara.

(**LEO** *stops typing.*)

I'm just a friend. A neighbor.

I've known her for like three weeks. Don't you remember? I…

And this isn't a fish for eating.

**LEO**. Then what the hell good is it?

**TOM**. It's a replacement fish.

**LEO**. *Replacement* fish?

**TOM**. To replace the fish she lost.

**LEO**. She lost her fish again, huh?

She's careless that way. Always has been.

**TOM**. No, no, they died. The tank water –?

**LEO**. She's always losing things.

She lost a husband the same way.

(**TOM** *just stares at* **LEO**, *surprised.*)

**LEO**. *(grabbing his wallet)* How much do I owe you?

**TOM**. No, Leo, I just dropped by to…

I was done with my shift so…

I thought I could run to the store for you guys. You know?

Get some necessities.

**LEO**. What kind of necessities?

**TOM.** I dunno, milk.

Bread.

Toilet paper.

**LEO.** You've known my daughter a couple weeks and already you're contemplating her bathroom habits?

**TOM.** Wasn't exactly *contemplating*.

**LEO.** Well, what *were* you doing?

**TOM.** …

Sara said she was gonna leave me a list.

**LEO.** *(He laughs.)* Have you seen her handwriting?

**TOM.** No.

**LEO.** Everything she writes looks like a doctor's prescription. Like a right-handed chimp writing left-handed…if the left hand had been crushed in a vise. *(beat)* That's why I gotta type it all up.

**TOM.** Leo…

**LEO.** What is it with the modern world? Zero regard for penmanship. It's a crime what they're *not* teaching in school these days.

**TOM.** *(news to him)* Sara's in school?

**LEO.** What time is it?

**TOM.** Eleven o'clock?

**LEO.** She better be. I used to play hooky when I was her age. It's a terrible habit.

**TOM.** *(confused)* Who are we talking about?

**LEO.** You tell me. You're the one who called this meeting.

**TOM.** I'm talking about Sara.

You said she was on the roof.

**LEO.** Don't quote me!

*(He tears the sheet of paper from the typewriter and hands it to TOM. TOM reads it.)*

**TOM.** What's this?

**LEO.** Sara's shopping list.

Read it back to me.

**TOM.** There's nothing on it.

**LEO**. So the first thing we need is ribbon.

    *(beat)*

    Say, you know what else we need?

    You know what we're *desperately* low on right at this instant?

**TOM**. Light bulbs?

**LEO**. Don't be an idiot!

    Mustard! The kind with the seeds!

    We never run out of light bulbs.

**TOM**. I was making a joke.

**LEO**. Leave that to the professionals.

    And get some bread while you're at it. Russian rye.

    My wife always lets the bread get stale.

    That's a firing offense as far as I'm concerned.

    *(**TOM** sets his goldfish down and heads to the kitchen area to look for a writing implement.)*

**TOM**. I should write this down.

**LEO**. Real men don't need lists!

**TOM**. *You* wrote it down.

**LEO**. No I didn't.

**TOM**. Sara's list?

**LEO**. What about it?

**TOM**. You typed it up.

**LEO**. You got any proof?

**TOM**. *(looking at blank paper)* You said...

**LEO**. Don't quote me!

    I don't need lists!

    *(tapping his forehead)* It's all right here.

    Real men keep it all right *here.*

    Can't you remember a few simple items?

    Typewriter ribbon. Russian rye. Mustard. The stuff you put in coffee.

**TOM**. Creamer?

**LEO.** Jesus Christ! Real men don't use creamer!!!

**TOM.** Okay.

**LEO.** I thought you claimed to be from Alaska?

**TOM.** I am from Alaska.

**LEO.** Is that why they asked you to leave?
I'm not talking about *creamer*, pal, I'm talkin' about the other thing...

**TOM.** Sugar.

**LEO.** You wanna get punched in the mouth?

**TOM.** What? No!

**LEO.** Then quit tryin' to annoy me.

**TOM.** *(trying to control his growing frustration)* I'm sorry, Leo! I just don't know what else goes in coffee besides cream and sugar.

*(SARA suddenly appears from the hallway. She's no longer relying on the crutches, but she's still wearing the orthopedic boot.)*

**SARA.** Cookies. He's talking about those little cookies you can dunk.

**LEO.** *(elementary)* Thank you!!!

**SARA.** The wafery kind. They're his favorite.

**TOM.** Your dad said you weren't home.

**SARA.** I'm home.

**TOM.** Your dad said you were on the roof.

**LEO.** I said don't quote me.
Don't *ever* quote me!

**TOM.** I'm totally confused.

**LEO.** They have pills for that.

**SARA.** Why are you here?

**LEO.** He wants to run errands...*apparently.*

**TOM.** You were gonna make a list?

**SARA.** Yeah, my foot was killing me so I took one of my pills and *wham.* *(Meaning: "Knocked me right out.")*

LEO. Give him something to do, will ya? He's driving me
nuts.

SARA. Be nice, Dad.

LEO. That's not my strong suit.
By the way, he's obsessed with your bathroom habits.

SARA. …?

TOM. No, no, I…

LEO. And he brought you a fish.

(TOM *holds up the goldfish.*)

A fish you can't eat.

TOM. I named him Frank.

(LEO *chuckles.*)

– But you can change it.

SARA. You bought me a fish?

LEO. We're not in the habit of naming the pets. I told him.

TOM. Sorry.

LEO. They're too unreliable.

(*Pause.* TOM *looks at* SARA.)

TOM. Can I ask you something?

(*She nods.*)

(*re:* LEO) In private?

(TOM *beckons her to join him across the room.* LEO *looks
in their direction.*)

LEO. (*like a bloodhound whiffing the scent*) What's this?

SARA. Dad, go to your room.

LEO. I will do no such thing. This is my house.

SARA. It's not your house.

LEO. For the record: I'm uncomfortable with the idea. Of
you. Alone. Out here. Unchaperoned. With Brad.

TOM. Tom.

SARA. I'm a grown woman, Dad.

LEO. That's what worries me.

**SARA.** Tom is perfectly harmless. *(turns to* **TOM***)* Right?

**TOM.** I guess. I mean, yes.

**SARA.** Okay: go ahead.

**TOM.** Um. Yeah. Here.

  *(He hands her the fish.)*

**SARA.** You bought me a fish.

**TOM.** Would you? …This is weird… *(Meaning: "With your dad right there.")*

**LEO.** I'm not listening.

  *(They both glance over at* **LEO***.)*

**TOM.** Would you like to, err… The thing is: go out with me?

  *(She really thinks about it.)*

**SARA.** *(matter-of-fact)* No.

**TOM.** This weekend?

**SARA.** No.

**TOM.** I got Saturday off.

  *(She thinks about it some more.)*

**SARA.** No.

**TOM.** For like a drink? Or a bite to eat? You could show me some of the hot spots.

**SARA.** Hotspots?

**TOM.** Yeah, the Denver nightlife.

**SARA.** I don't know any hotspots.

**TOM.** Didn't you say you'd lived in Denver your whole life?

**LEO.** *Strikeout!*

**SARA.** Shut up, Dad!

**TOM.** So, what do you say?

**SARA.** I'm still not very mobile. You'd basically have to fireman's lift me all over downtown, and that wouldn't be any fun for either of us, so…

**TOM.** No, yeah, I thought about that.

I told my supervisor about your little accident, and he said it was cool if I borrowed a wheelchair from the airport.

**SARA.** You told your supervisor about me?

**LEO.** Uh-oh!

**TOM.** Well, I couldn't just take it without authori –

**SARA.** I can't leave my dad.

**LEO.** I can't be trusted.

**SARA.** And I don't really like to, you know, go out.
In public.

**TOM.** Well, what if –?

**LEO.** Are you deaf? She said: No!

**SARA.** Dad.

**TOM.** What if I made you dinner? You *and* your dad.

**LEO.** That sounds like a terrible idea.

**TOM.** I'm a pretty good cook, actually. Make a mean seafood stew.

**LEO.** Jesus, this guy is *dim*. I told you she was allergic.

**TOM.** I thought he was just...

**SARA.** No, actually I am. Shrimp, shellfish, I just balloon right up.

**TOM.** Then something really basic: spaghetti.

**LEO.** I'm allergic to spaghetti.

**SARA.** No, you're not!

**TOM.** I make my own sauce.

**LEO.** I'm *really* allergic to sauce.

**SARA.** I don't know.

**TOM.** *(a sweetener)* I got some nice local wine as a going away present.

**LEO.** Nice wine?

**TOM.** Yeah.

**LEO.** As a present?

**TOM.** Uhuh.

**LEO.** From your friends?

**TOM.** Yeah.

**LEO.** In Alaska? Nice local *Alaskan* wine?

Thanks, but no thanks, Chef Boyardee!

**SARA.** Tom: don't take this the wrong way.

**TOM.** Okay?

**LEO.** Tell him.

**SARA.** I'm – this is –

**TOM.** What?

**LEO.** – Tell him already.

**SARA.** Dad, would you please butt out.

**TOM.** No, it's okay. I'm sorry. This wasn't cool of me to just barge in here and think that – I don't exactly know what I was thinking but I think I was thinking that maybe – I do this, actually, a lot, I manufacture scenarios that have no basis in reality, it's probably because I have a job where there's a lot of standing around, so… I'm gonna go. Enjoy your fish. Have a good night.

**LEO.** We *were.*

**SARA.** Tom, wait a second.

(**SARA** *tries to beat him to the doorway and ends up losing her balance and falling.* **TOM** *rushes to her aid.*)

| **SARA.** | **TOM.** | **LEO.** |
|---|---|---|
| Ow, shit! Shit. | | |
| | Oh my god, are you okay? | What happened? What's going on? |
| No, no, no. | | |
| | That was my fault. | What did you do? |
| He didn't do anything, dad. | | You son of a bitch! |
| Dad, I fell. | | |
| | | He pushed you? |

**SARA.** I'm okay, it's fine. I just, sometimes I forget about this *stupid…!!!!*

**TOM**. Here, put your arm around me.

**LEO**. Oh, would you stop being so *obvious.*

**TOM**. I'm trying to help her up.

**LEO**. I know what you're trying! Mr. Nice Guy!

**SARA**. Please, dad.

**TOM**. I am nice.

**LEO**. That's what they all say!

**TOM**. *(coming out much more emphatically than he intends)* Okay, look, I'm taking this damn list *(He grabs* **SARA***'s shopping list that has nothing on it.)* and getting everything on it, *plus* the fixings for dinner, alright? And then I'm coming back over here Saturday night to make you, *both* of you, a nice home-cooked meal. *(to* **LEO***)* It won't kill you to choke down a glass of local Alaskan wine, either. And if you don't like the sound of that, you… you can eat your supper in your room. *(to* **SARA***)* That's it, no more discussion. Executive decision. Are there any questions?

*(CRASH!!!!!!!!!!!! A hockey puck smashes through the apartment window, billowing the drapes, hitting a lamp and blowing out the bulb.* **TOM***'s training kicks in – he hits the deck. Several light bulbs in the room flicker and go out.* **LEO** *and* **SARA** *remain totally unfazed by this.)*

Jesus Christ!!!!!

**LEO**. Plywood!

**TOM**. What?

**LEO**. Bread, mustard, cookies, *plywood.* Add it to the list, *Brad.*

*(blackout)*

## Four

*(Saturday night. It is raining. The buckets around the
room are catching drips from the ceiling. We hear a
soft, intermittent "blip-blip" throughout the scene. It's a
pleasant sound.* **TOM***, wearing an apron and his "good
shirt," is sinking a last screw into a sheet of plywood
covering the window.* **SARA** *has her feet up on the couch.
Dinner is over, and they are each nursing glasses of
wine –* **SARA***'s is in a plastic cup, of course. Frank, the
goldfish, is in a small bowl on the coffee table, swimming
around. Mid-conversation:)*

**SARA.** I just ate my own body weight in vermicelli!

**TOM.** What you think of the sauce?

**SARA.** Your mother taught you well.

**TOM.** It wasn't my mother.

I was married for a couple years. She loved to cook.

*(He looks over at her expectantly, fishing.)* What about you?

**SARA.** I wish I could cook.

**TOM.** No, I mean, were you ever married?

*(She tastes some more of the sauce.)*

**SARA.** Okay, I really, really should stop eating.

**TOM.** I'll give you the recipe. The trick is to roast the garlic
before-hand. Sweetens it right up. And only use fresh
oregano.

**SARA.** No, I can't cook.

**TOM.** It's a piece a cake.

**SARA.** No, I mean I *can't* cook. Things catch on fire.

**TOM.** You're kidding?

*(She's not kidding.)*

**SARA.** So this is a treat. We usually eat sandwiches. Salads.
Things that don't require, y'know, heat.

**TOM.** You *are* kidding, right?

*(She shakes her head. He sits beside her on the couch,
grabs his wine.)*

**TOM**. When was the last time you had a hot meal?

**SARA**. Well...I do remember exactly what I was eating.

**TOM**. Okay?

**SARA**. It was a pork chop.

**TOM**. Uhuh.

**SARA**. With creamed corn.

**TOM**. Yeah?

**SARA**. And the fluffiest mashed potatoes I have *ever* tasted in my entire life. And I was watching TV. And I remember thinking to myself, "Oh my god, I am actually watching history in the making!"

**TOM**. What was on TV?

**SARA**. The fall of the Berlin Wall.

*(a beat)*

**TOM**. You haven't had a hot meal since 1989???

*(She shakes her head. **TOM** has no idea what to say.)*

Well...I fix this a couple times a week, so...I'll make extra next time and box some up for you and your dad. You *can* microwave, right? *(He chuckles.)* Without burning the place down?

**SARA**. Yeah. Of course.

**TOM**. Okay. Good.

**SARA**. But it gives me headaches.

I have EHS: electromagnetic hypersensitivity.

It's pretty rare.

I also can't use a blow dryer.

Or a cellphone.

And garage doors are something of a problem, so...

*(She smiles and takes a sip of wine.)*

*(silence)*

**TOM**. This is a weird date.

**SARA**. It's not really a date.

**TOM**. It's sort of a date. It has all the date-like features.

SARA. No. Like what?

TOM. Like wine? Like I made you dinner? *(re: his shirt)* I ironed.

SARA. Like you just boarded up my window with a sheet of plywood?

TOM. Like that moment when you tried to grab the parmesan cheese...and I tried to grab the parmesan cheese at exactly the same time, and there was that *thing* that happened?

SARA. What thing?

TOM. You know: that thing?

SARA. No.

TOM. That undeniable...whatchamacallit?

SARA. Fight over the parmesan cheese?

TOM. I don't what you'd call it, but it was...probably a French word.

SARA. French?

TOM. Yeah, the French just have more words to describe these sorta things.

SARA. The French do?

TOM. Uhuh.

SARA. I'm pretty sure we have more words than the French.

TOM. I've seen it in French movies where the whole thing takes place in a restaurant, and they're smoking, and there's just this apparent understanding that things are *progressing*...

SARA. We're not in a restaurant.

TOM. I'm just saying I was aware of the acute date-like moment thing. It was huge. And it was French. That's all I'm saying.

*(He sips his wine happily.)*

SARA. Can we not call it a date?

TOM. Even if, for you, it was more subtle.

**SARA**. Are we still talking about parmesan cheese?

**TOM**. How about "pre-date." Can we call it a pre-date? Are you comfortable with the term "pre-date?"

**SARA**. Pre-date?

**TOM**. Like a practice date.

**SARA**. Let's change the subject.

*(With his napkin,* **TOM** *picks up the hockey puck that did all the damage in the last scene like a CSI investigator.)*

**TOM**. *(gesturing with it)* Hockey puck! *This* could have knocked somebody's teeth out. You should report it to the police. They could dust for prints.

**SARA**. *(matter-of-fact)* Oh, I know his folks.

**TOM**. You know who did this? Call the cops.

**SARA**. *(don't be silly)* No one's ever been hit. It makes a mess, but it gives me something to do around the house all day.

*(***TOM** *just stares at* **SARA**, *then at the puck.)*

**TOM**. What should I do with it?

**SARA**. Just put it with the others. *(pointing)* The closet?

*(***TOM** *opens the closet. Sporting goods come spilling out: baseball, tennis balls, lots of hockey pucks, etc.)*

**TOM**. This has happened before?

**SARA**. Happens all the time.
He lives across the street, actually, in your building.
He's a sweet kid.

**TOM**. This is the…? All of this, the same k –?

**SARA**. He always comes to apologize, and it's so cute, he's terrified of my dad.

*(***TOM** *recognizes the feeling.)*

His mom sends over cookies.

**TOM**. Well, he better not bust my front window, I tell ya that much.

**SARA.** He's never broken anyone else's window on the
    block.

It's just me.

Lucky me!

It's the only way I get fresh-baked cookies around here.

(**TOM** *is feeling sort of useless.*)

**TOM.** *(misplaced machismo)* You want me to talk to him?

You want me to put the screws to him?

Kids respond to the uniform.

**SARA.** *(smiling)* Oh, yeah?

**TOM.** Not really.

**SARA.** Why would you want to talk to him?

**TOM.** Protect your interests.

**SARA.** My interests are protected just fine.

(*He drinks his wine. They sit in silence for a moment –
just the "blip-blip" from the leaky roof.*)

You were married?

**TOM.** Uhuh.

What about you?

**SARA.** Why'd you get divorced?

**TOM.** *(oddly, sadly)* I can't remember.

(*Silence.* **TOM** *looks up at the leaky ceiling.*)

Drip, drip, drip.

(*She laughs. They look at each other. Are they going to
kiss?*)

Are you sure?

**SARA.** What?

**TOM.** Because I could have sworn…

**SARA.** What?

**TOM.** The thing…before…with the parmesan: that you
    wanted to…that you wanted me to…

**SARA.** Uhuh?

**TOM.** Kiss me/you.

SARA. Why would I do that?

TOM. Err…

SARA. I mean why would I do that on a pre-date?

TOM. So this *is* a pre-date?

SARA. Why would I *theoretically* kiss you on an alleged pre-date?

TOM. Alleged?

SARA. I mean that's not even an initial date-like feature, is it? I mean, seriously? That's more of a second date-like feature? Right?

   *(beat)*

TOM. Should I change the subject again?

SARA. Please.

TOM. Where d'you keep the fish food?

SARA. Under the sink.
   Next to the cat food.

   (**TOM** *grabs the fish food and crosses back to the couch.*)

TOM. You know: I've yet to see this so-called cat.

SARA. Tell me about it.

TOM. *(dropping food in the bowl)* Okay, Frank. Dinner time, little buddy.

SARA. *(almost sternly)* Please don't call him that. If I get attached it's just going to be harder when he dies.

TOM. How do you know he'll die?

SARA. Wherever I put the fish tank…it doesn't matter how often I move it, the ceiling springs a leak and it starts dripping, like within half-hour, like clockwork.

TOM. Well, so far so good.

SARA. He'll die. It's only a matter of time.

TOM. I picked a pretty healthy looking guy. I *think* he's a guy.

SARA. He will die. They all die. They all disappear. The longest any pet ever survived me is like three months.

TOM. Then why do you even have pets?
   Why not have plants?

**SARA.** They get fruit flies. All kinds of weird diseases. What's the opposite of a green thumb?

*(They sit for a moment in silence, watching the fish.)*

**TOM.** *(re: Frank)* Look at him go!

**SARA.** Do you think it's callous of me? To keep replacing them? Knowing what I know?

**TOM.** What is it you know?

**SARA.** *(Instead of answering,* **SARA** *offers this:)* My mother used to keep fish. It was my job to feed them when I got home from school. Dad would come home from work and sit in his armchair and just stare at the fish for hours to calm his nerves.

**TOM.** It's too bad he can't see 'em anymore.

**SARA.** He feels them.

*(a beat)*

**TOM.** What did he do?

**SARA.** Ran a little insurance business. For 45 years.

**TOM.** See, there it was again.

**SARA.** What?

**TOM.** You said the word "insurance" and your mouth did this weird thing.

**SARA.** No it didn't.

**TOM.** That French thing. You didn't feel that?

**SARA.** Change the subject.

**TOM.** We should confront it.

**SARA.** I'm not confronting something *French* my mouth did when I said the word "insurance."

**TOM.** Don't freak out. I'm just going to lean in, slowly, and give you a pre-kiss. It's not a real kiss.

*(He leans in, slowly.)*

**SARA.** Okay. What do I do?

**TOM.** It's the same set-up, basically…

*(She leans forward, slowly, just as…)*

(**LEO**, *in his pajamas, enters carrying his dirty dishes. He goes straight to the sink, dumps them, indignantly, takes a roll of toilet paper from a grocery bag on the counter, turns around and heads right back out of the room, toilet paper held high above his head in silent protest.*)

You know, I was just kidding around when I told him he should go to his room to eat dinner.

**SARA**. Don't worry about it.

**TOM**. I think I got off on the wrong foot with your dad.

**SARA**. There's no right foot.

(*a beat*)

**TOM**. He seems pretty healthy.

For a guy his age.

Physically, I mean.

He's confused about a lot of things, though.

He thinks my name is Brad.

(*brief pause*)

Does he even know anyone named Brad?

(*brief pause*)

He thinks his wife is still alive. She's not, right?

(**SARA** *shakes her head, 'No.'*)

He said you were married. Were you married?

**SARA**. Is there more wine?

(*He empties the bottle into their glasses.*)

**TOM**. And then he said –

**SARA**. Tom.

**TOM**. I think he sometimes thinks you're still a kid.

He said you were in school.

You're not in school-school, are you? Like grad school?

**SARA**. No, Tom –

**TOM**. (*one long breath*) Or do you teach? Because you look like a teacher. I thought that the first second I saw you,

I said, I wonder if she's a teacher? Where do you teach? Do you teach? I mean what do you do? Do you work? How do you live? How do you guys survive? What's up with your dad? Where is your cat? Were you married, Sara? Who is Brad?

**SARA.** *(sharply)* This has been nice.

We should do it again.

In a couple weeks.

But it would be really, really, really great if you didn't ask me so many questions. I just have this thing about…

**TOM.** Questions?

**SARA.** Yeah.

**TOM.** Okay.

    *(**TOM** gets out his wallet, takes out a twenty.)*

Twenty bucks.

**SARA.** What's this?

**TOM.** You said "*survive.*" The longest "any pet ever survived" you was three months. Kind of a weird thing to say, don't you think? Sorry, that was another question. Okay: a statement. Twenty bucks says Frank here makes it to the Fourth of July.

**SARA.** He won't.

**TOM.** I say he will.

**SARA.** I don't like the Fourth of July.

**TOM.** But your dad does. He was pissed he missed the fireworks.

**SARA.** I don't like fireworks.

**TOM.** Then the *Fifth* of July. Twenty bucks little Frankie makes it to the Fifth.

**SARA.** It's not gonna happen.

**TOM.** Put your money where your mouth is.

    *(He lifts his glass.)*

    *(She looks at him. Beat.)*

    *(They clink glasses together. **TOM**'s glass shatters.)*

    *(blackout)*

# ACT TWO

## One

*(Several months later.* **LEO** *is alone on the couch. He appears to be on the phone, his papers scattered on the coffee table in front of him. His necktie is loosened; his shirtsleeves are rolled up. There is a workman's stepladder just inside the kitchen area. After a few moments, there is a knock at the door.* **LEO** *ignores it. Another knock.* **LEO** *ignores it. A third, slightly louder knock.)*

**LEO.** Go away!!!

**TOM.** *(off)* It's Tom.

**LEO.** Who?

**TOM.** *(off)* You know who it is.

**LEO.** No I don't.

**TOM.** *(off)* I bring you food? I've been coming round for a couple months now. Can I come in?

**LEO.** What are you selling?

**TOM.** *(off)* It won't take long.

*(another soft knock)*

**LEO.** I'm on the phone with a client.

**TOM.** *(off)* I need to see Sara, can you open the door?

**LEO.** She said she didn't wanna see you again.

**TOM.** *(off)* No she didn't.

I'm not leaving until I see her.

**LEO.** She's not here.

**TOM.** *(off)* Are you lying?

> *(a beat)*

> Leo…?

> **(LEO** *reluctantly shuffles to the door and unlocks it.* **TOM** *enters.)*

**TOM.** Hi.

**LEO.** *(covering receiver with his palm)* Sssh!

> **(TOM** *looks around the room.)*

**TOM.** *(indicating off)* Is she…?

**LEO.** Look, I'm trying to run a business here. You can't just drop by unannounced. You need to call ahead for an appointment. She's in a meeting.

**TOM.** What meeting?

**LEO.** You'll have to wait. Read a magazine.

> **(TOM** *looks around: there are no magazines.)*

**TOM.** I'm late for work already.

**LEO.** Whaddaya want, a note?

**TOM.** I thought you were on the phone.

**LEO.** I *am* on the phone.

> **(LEO** *just stands there with the receiver to his ear.)*

**TOM.** Who you talking to?

**LEO.** *(none of your…)* It's a *business* call.

> **(LEO** *just stands there with the receiver to his ear some more.)*

**TOM.** Is anyone on the line? Leo?

**LEO.** I'm on hold, moron.

> *(Pause.* **TOM** *looks at his watch.)*

**TOM.** Look, do you mind if I just – ?

**LEO.** You can't go back there.

**TOM.** *(drifting toward hallway)* It'll just take a s –

**LEO.** She's in the can.

**TOM.** You said she was in a meeting.

**LEO.** Well, *Brad*, where I come from we try to be discreet about these things. How would you like it if every time *you* had the urge, they made an airport-wide announcement: "Ladies and Gentlemen, we need to temporarily suspend the screening process while one of our crack-a-jack agents goes potty"?

*(a beat)*

**TOM.** Why do you do that?

Why do you insist on calling me Brad?

**LEO.** What would you like to be called?

**TOM.** You know it's not my name.

**LEO.** I do?

**TOM.** Stop it, okay, stop doing that, stop acting dumb. You know *exactly* what my name is.

**LEO.** Are you sure?

**TOM.** You know more than you pretend to know.

I think maybe… Okay, I understand that *some* things are *slipping* for you. I get that. And I'm very sorry that that's happening to you, Leo, I am really, that must be…frustrating… But I think you know a whole lot more than you let on.

**LEO.** Interesting theory.

**TOM.** Yeah.

**LEO.** Like what?

Can you give me an example?

**TOM.** Huh?

**LEO.** Of some of these things I'm supposed to know but am pretending not to.

**TOM.** Err…

**LEO.** Because I'm acting dumb.

**TOM.** Well…

**LEO.** It's a pretty flimsy argument…unless you can back it up with some hard evidence.

**TOM.** You've got selective memory.

**LEO.** Selective memory? Now, what is that again?

**TOM.** You remember whatever's convenient.

**LEO.** Look: Brad…

**TOM.** You've been calling me Brad, but you *remembered* I worked for TSA.

**LEO.** Is that the chicken place?

**TOM.** I've told you a *million* times my name's Tom.

**LEO.** Look, buddy, I can't be expected to keep track of every little detail. I have an office to run.

**TOM.** You don't have an office.

**LEO.** What's this?

**TOM.** It's a file folder on your daughter's coffee table in your daughter's apartment. Sara told me. You retired. Years ago.

**LEO.** Then what am I doing on the phone with our most important client? Huh? Columbo?

(*brief pause*)

**TOM.** There's nobody on that phone. You're full of shit, Leo.

**LEO.** There's no one on this phone?

**TOM.** Don't think so.

**LEO.** I'm full of shit? You break into my home – ?

**TOM.** You invited me.

**LEO.** – And tell me I'm full of shit?

**TOM.** I didn't *break* in. And it's not your home.

**LEO.** You barge in here…in your stupid uniform and your little toy badge –

**TOM.** It's not stupid –

**LEO.** – Throwin' your weight around like some…

**TOM.** I took an oath, okay?

**LEO.** An oath!!! Well then.

**TOM.** As a federal employee, and I…
    Wait. How do you know I'm in uniform?

**LEO.** BECAUSE I CAN SMELL IT! Haven't you heard that? When you're deprived of one of your senses, all the others become *super*-sensitive, a heightened awareness.

**TOM.** You can smell my uniform?

**LEO.** I can *smell* your uniform and *hear* that stupid look on your face. Sight is the most overrated sense there is. I don't need to see you're in uniform, you *told* me...you told me you were late for work, Sherlock!

**TOM.** So you *do* know I work at the airport.

**LEO.** I just know you're in uniform.

**TOM.** Because you can smell it?

**LEO.** Because I know you're not a cop.

**TOM.** How do you know that?

**LEO.** Because you don't have a gun.

**TOM.** What makes you so sure I don't have a gun?

**LEO.** If you had a gun you'da shot me already.

*(We hear a toilet flush.)*

**TOM.** Sara!

**LEO.** Keep your voice down.

**TOM.** Give me that phone. Give it to me!

**LEO.** I'm on hold!

**TOM.** There's no one on the line!

*(**LEO** holds out the receiver, calls his bluff.)*

**LEO.** *(with sudden vehemence)* You wanna talk to the client? You wanna explain how the policy works?
You wanna be responsible when disaster befalls her family and she's not covered because she *forgot to check* the little box and mail it back to the head office? Huh? Mr. Security? Mr. I Took An Oath???

*(**TOM** just stands there, abashed.)*

*(silence)*

**TOM.** Is she ever coming out of there?

**LEO.** That's kinda personal, don't you think?

*(pause)*

**TOM.** I had an epiphany.

**LEO.** Well, that must be very nice for you.

**TOM**. I really need to talk with her, Leo.

**LEO**. Then talk. She can hear you. You can hear every word back there. The walls are like paper. G'head. We have conversations all the time while we're in the can.

**TOM**. You do?

**LEO**. Lengthy conversations. Meaningful discourse. Every topic under the sun. Go ahead. Whatever it is: get it off your chest.

**TOM**. *(tentatively calling off)* Sara?

**LEO**. G'head, she's listening.

> *(***TOM*** *looks at* **LEO** *distrustfully.)*

Go ahead, I'm otherwise engaged.

> *(***LEO*** *focuses on his call, his paperwork.* **TOM** *takes a step toward the bedrooms. This is not the way he saw this going down. He turns shyly away from Leo, trying to gain a little privacy.)*

**TOM**. *(calls off, louder than he would prefer)* Hi.

It's Tom.

I was getting ready for work.

I couldn't get my tie straight. I've got this supervisor who's sort of a dick about these things, so I'm looking in the mirror and I'm staring at myself staring in the mirror, wrestling with this *clip*, and I was like: what did Sara have for breakfast? I wonder if she's wearing something blue today?

I was spacing out. Thinking about you.

I think about you all the time…

> *(***LEO*** *lets out a long-suffering sigh.)*

…and I have this, um…*urge*, I guess, frequently, to tell you stuff, and I…*spew*. Things I haven't told anyone before. Because I feel safe, weirdly, around you. Is that weird? Am I talking too much? I don't know what that is, but I think it's a good thing. So: so: I wanted to say…

> *(He looks over at* **LEO**.*)*

**LEO**. *(on phone)* Yes, I can keep holding.

**TOM.** …that I have *feelings* for you.

(*Off, a toilet flushes, again.*)

I haven't had *said feelings* in a long…time. I've kinda been in "shut-down" mode. But you make me want to be… *Doing* stuff. With you. On a semi-regular basis. Things of a date-like nature. Without other people around. That's it.

That's all I wanted to say.

Sara?

(*At once from the hallway comes* **YURI**, *a middle-aged Ukrainian man in a neck brace and overalls.* **TOM** *stares at him confusedly.*)

**YURI.** I can't find problem with lights.

**TOM.** Who are you?

**YURI.** I am Yuri.

**TOM.** Who?

**YURI.** I am the landlord.

**TOM.** Where's Sara?

**YURI.** Who are you?

**LEO.** That's Brad.

**TOM.** I'm Tom.

**YURI.** The boyfriend?

**LEO.** Over my dead body!

**YURI.** (*to* **LEO**) It's not the wiring.

**TOM.** You said she was back there.

**LEO.** What do I look like, her secretary?

**TOM.** (*audible/inaudible*) Faaaaaaaaaggghhhh!

**YURI.** There's nothing wrong with fuses. It's just one-a those things, yeah? And you're out of toilet paper. Okay, I gotta go. I come back later fix window.

(**YURI** *goes to grab his stepladder.* **TOM** *grabs the phone from* **LEO** *and listens.*)

**TOM.** I can't believe you! There's nobody on the damned line, Leo!

**LEO.** That's AT&T for you!

**TOM.** You're just fucking with me!

*(He slams the receiver down really hard.)*

**YURI.** *(to TOM)* Is there problem?

**TOM.** No... Yuri...there's no problem... Leo here just enjoys *fucking* with anyone who's the least bit kind to his daughter...which, from what I can tell, hasn't happened in a hell of a long time, so he should be thankful that someone's shown a bit of interest.

*(There's a silence in the room. TOM is suddenly aware of what he's said.)*

That didn't come out right.

*(The moment is punctuated by the phone which starts ringing.)*

**LEO.** If it's for me take a message.

*(LEO starts to exit. TOM snatches up the phone.)*

**TOM.** What??? Sara?

*(LEO turns back.)*

**LEO.** Tell her about the epiphany.

**YURI.** He had an epiphany?

**LEO.** *(an explanation, oddly)* He's a federal employee.

**TOM.** Yeah, I hung up on you. I didn't know it was you, your dad said you were at a meeting.

You are at a meeting. Okay. How did you...?

It's not a bother, you should have asked.

Give me the clinic's address.

*(to LEO)* I need a pen.

**LEO.** We don't have pens.

They run out of ink.

*(He gestures to YURI to help him find something to write it down on. But YURI sits in front of LEO's typewriter.)*

**TOM**. 810 East Harvard.

> (**YURI** *types.*)

I'm late anyway, I'll just call in sick.

**LEO**. *(throwing up his hands)* One less guardian at the gate!

> (**LEO** *exits.* **TOM** *hangs up.* **YURI** *tears the sheet of paper from the typewriter and hands it to* **TOM**.)

**TOM**. That was Sara.

**YURI**. Okay.

**TOM**. I have to go get her.

**YURI**. Okay.

**TOM**. I thought he was bullshitting.

**YURI**. Okay.

**TOM**. How can I possibly forge a bond with her father if I can't tell if he's bullshitting?

**YURI**. Do what I do.

Divide by three.

Whatever he says: you take: you divide by three.

**TOM**. What?

**YURI**. I figure this out: whatever come out Leo's mouth, approximately one out of three things is true, one out of three, he not remember, one of out of three, is complete, utter bullshit.

**TOM**. But how do you know which?

**YURI**. Don't think it matters. But sure makes it easier to get along with him.

> (**YURI** *puts stepladder over his shoulder and starts for the door.*)

Hey, Tom. It's Tom, right? I give you some of advice for free, yes?

**TOM**. That's okay.

**YURI**. I give it anyway.

Don't go out with her.

That's my thinking.

**TOM**. Thanks. Why not?

**YURI**. It's a nice speech…the speech you give, it's nice…if you give me this speech I see you are serious contender, but Sara? Is different.

**TOM**. What, why?

**YURI**. There's complexity. There's…what they say in Hollywood… "Back Story." Don't go out with her. Trust me.

**TOM**. Listen, Yuri…

**YURI**. And if you do… It's not my place.

**TOM**. No, what, what?

**YURI**. *(ominously)* Be careful.

**TOM**. I don't follow.

**YURI**. I put my mouth where my foot is. Sorry. I go now.

**TOM**. Listen, thanks, but we've actually already been on a date, so:

  (**YURI** *stops in his tracks.*)

**YURI**. A date?

**TOM**. I was just ratcheting the whole thing up, you know?

**YURI**. Ratcheting?

**TOM**. Yeah.

**YURI**. To the next level?

**TOM**. Uhuh.

**YURI**. Up from date?

**TOM**. Right.

**YURI**. Because you are positive original situation you speak of was *date*?

**TOM**. Pretty sure.

**YURI**. She called it 'a date?'

**TOM**. Well, no.

**YURI**. You made it clear to her it was 'date?'

**TOM**. Not exactly.

**YURI**. Okay, this is what I'm saying, this is critical, Tom. This is: what they say in Hollywood: "Major Plot Point." Where did you go?

**TOM.** Go?

**YURI.** What restaurant? What movie?

**TOM.** Nowhere. Here. She didn't want to leave her dad.

**YURI.** Okay, good, this is what I'm saying: she doesn't leave the house –? Don't be worried.

**TOM.** She leaves the house.

**YURI.** No.

**TOM.** She sometimes leaves the house. Why would I be worried?

**YURI.** When?

Can you give example?

**TOM.** Today. She went to the doctor.

**YURI.** The doctor?

**TOM.** To look at her foot. She's getting the boot off.

**YURI.** So this is what she *has* to do, not what she *wants* to do.

**TOM.** Okay, look:

**YURI.** You worry me for a second. You were having me think you went on date, like *outside*, but now I see, you're fine, no problem. Just…don't go out with her. This was nice talk we had. Can you get door?

(**TOM** *starts to open the door for* **YURI**.)

It's none of my business.

**TOM.** Okay.

**YURI.** It's a free country. It's…what they say in Hollywood…?

**TOM.** *(firmly)* Do you have something you wanna say?

**YURI.** I do not like putting my nose in the business of others.

**TOM.** Yuri!

**YURI.** *(building, increasingly ominous)* Be careful. Okay?

Things happen.

To people.

That hang around.

I wouldn't want to see you get hurt.

**YURI**. *(cont.)* Like I got hurt.

Or Brad.

**TOM**. What are you talking about?

**YURI**. Ask her about her husband. Do you know this?

Ask her about Brad.

And the one after. And the one after that.

I've said too much already.

**TOM**. No, no, no, Yuri –

**YURI**. You're nice guy, I'm sorry. I go now. I fix window later.

**TOM**. Hold on a second!

(**TOM** *grabs* **YURI** *roughly by the arm.*)

**YURI**. Sara is *Likho*.

(*He spits twice.*)

This is a word we have. In Ukraine.

(*a beat*)

I ask her for coffee last year. Innocent coffee, like friends, yes? I come to fetch her, I fall on steps, almost break neck.

(**YURI** *indicates his neck brace.*)

**TOM**. That was months ago, why you still wearing that?

**YURI**. Just in case!!!

**TOM**. Okay.

**YURI**. You don't get it. That was Sara.

**TOM**. That's ridiculous. It's a coincidence.

**YURI**. *(prophetically)* There is no coincidence.

(**YURI** *puts down the ladder and unbuckles his overalls.*)

**TOM**. Okay, whoa, whoa…

(**YURI** *pulls down the waist of his pants and reveals a scar on his hip.*)

**YURI**. Dog bite: yes? Carrying Sara's groceries home from King Soopers.

(*He pushes back his hair, indicates another scar.*)

Sara's windows, I am cleaning. I make bucket of soapy water in yard. I turn on hose, it snakes around feet of ladder. Ladder slides right off siding, strikes me *here*. I am unconscious six hours. What, you don't believe me? Ask Leo.

TOM. No, it's just…

YURI. My truck. My Toyota truck. Ask Leo. Takes me six years to pay off. The day I make final payment, it catch fire, no joke, last year, middle of the night. What was I doing? Nothing/sleeping. What did I do *that day*? *(re: couch)* Help Sara move this couch she buy downtown.

*(a beat)*

And Juanita Suarez.

TOM. Juanita Suarez?

YURI. My mother's cat. She go to Florida every year to visit sister.

TOM. The cat?

YURI. No, my *mother*! She give me cat. I cannot have cat because of allergy. I give cat to Sara to live for one, two, few days here in apartment. I drop off Juanita Suarez with her scratching post and her fishy treats, and this is last we ever see of Juanita Suarez. *(He gestures with his hands – the mysterious disappearance of Juanita Suarez.)* Pphhhttt!
Sara. I love her, okay, but she is Likho.

*(YURI spits.)*

TOM. What the hell does that mean?

YURI. Bad luck.

*(YURI turns to leave. Before he leaves, he points an oddly threatening finger at TOM, and spits twice. As the door closes shut, one, two, three, several light bulbs fizzle out.)*

*(blackout)*

## Two

(**YURI** *has just finished replacing the broken glass in the window. He's putting the finishing touches on the putty around the new pane.* **LEO** *is on the couch, a sandwich on a plate before him. With a ridiculously large carving knife he carefully cuts the sandwich in half, and is about to take a bite, when…*)

**YURI.** Okidoke! Is fixed.

**LEO.** Finally. It's been six months.

**YURI.** Not six.

**LEO.** I have a keen sense of the passage of time.

**YURI.** Whatever you say, boss.

**LEO.** What do you do all day?

**YURI.** You have no idea the responsibility landlording building like this.

**LEO.** It's not Versailles, pal. There are four units.

**YURI.** They're *big* units.

**LEO.** And you live in one of 'em.

**YURI.** Three *big* units. Everyday it's something else, the dishwasher, the waste disposal, I can't keep up with you people. The paperwork alone…

**LEO.** Don't tell me about paperwork!

**YURI.** The others? Easy tenants; pieces of cake. But you? And Sara? How many times I fix window? Huh, Leo? How many?

**LEO.** I'm not a mathematician.

**YURI.** Try six. Six times I fix window. In last year *alone.* Every month I fix leaky ceiling.

**LEO.** It's not fixed. You call that fixed?

**YURI.** Because leak keeps moving!

**LEO.** *(waving the knife in* **YURI**'s *direction)* How is that my problem?

(**YURI** *crosses to the kitchen to wash his hands.*)

**YURI.** Why you in such pissy mood?

**LEO**. This is my baseline mood.

**YURI**. Because Sara is with the security guard?

**LEO**. Shut up, Yuri!

**YURI**. Take it easy. What they say in Hollywood, "Don't get angry with landlord."

(**LEO** *settles on the couch to eat his sandwich.* **YURI** *notices a plate of cookies on the counter.*)

Are these *the* cookies?

**LEO**. What cookies?

**YURI**. The kid's mom bakes the cookies? The window kid?

**LEO**. Those are the cookies.

**YURI**. Can I have a cookie?

**LEO**. You don't deserve a cookie.

**YURI**. I fix window!

**LEO**. Took you six months to fix my window.

**YURI**. It's not your window.

**LEO**. Took you six months to fix my daughter's window.

**YURI**. Not six.

**LEO**. Six months!

**YURI**. *(does the math under his breath)* Divide by three!

**LEO**. What?

**YURI**. Nothing.

Please, Leo, I'm hungry. I didn't eat today.

**LEO**. You're Ukrainian. You should be used to it.

**YURI**. Can I have sandwich?

**LEO**. The bread's stale.

**YURI**. *(peering into fridge)* Can I have leftovers?

**LEO**. What leftovers?

**YURI**. In Tupperware with note.

*(reading the note)* "My secret recipe. Enjoy. Tom."

Can I have?

**LEO**. Be my guest.

(**YURI** *puts the leftovers in a pot on the stove.*)

*(The front door suddenly flies open, and* **SARA** *and* **TOM** *stagger into the room.* **TOM** *has his arm in a sling and there's a bandage around his head with a spot of blood seeping through it.* **SARA** *guides him toward a chair. She no longer wears the orthopedic boot on her foot.)*

**SARA.** Can I get some help here?

**YURI.** *(coming to assist)* Isus Khrystos, shcho trapylosya? *(Meaning: "Jesus Christ, what happened?)*

**TOM.** It's okay, I'm okay.

**SARA.** You're not okay.

**LEO.** *(cheerfully)* How was the date?

**YURI.** What did you do?

**SARA.** Mini-putting.

**YURI.** Dangerous sport.

*(quickly, under this breath)* Likho! *(Spits twice.)*

Is it broken?

**LEO.** *(gleefully)* Something's broken?

**TOM.** Dislocated. I'm fine.

It was a misunderstanding.

**LEO.** That's what they all say.

**SARA.** He got hit. Over the head. With a golf club. Twice.

*(***YURI*** *spits again.* **LEO** *laughs then takes a bite of his sandwich.)*

It's not funny.

**YURI.** Who hit you?

**SARA.** A six year old.

**LEO.** That's funny.

**SARA.** He had to have stitches, dad.

**TOM.** I'm fine.

**SARA.** Nine stitches.

**LEO.** Really funny!

**YURI.** Looks bad.

**TOM.** It looks worse than it is.

**YURI.** Still looks bad.

**TOM.** Do you have any Tylenol?

**LEO.** We're fresh out.

**SARA.** No we're not. Yuri?

(*YURI goes off to the bathroom and returns with pills.*)

**LEO.** Oh boy, I'm dying to hear this little yarn.

**TOM.** The kid was swinging his club a little wildly and lost his grip, that's all. No biggie. I just went over to tell him to be careful, and –

**SARA.** The kid's mother.

**TOM.** – Thought I was, you know, menacing her son, I guess. So:

**SARA.** She hit him with her club.

(*LEO chuckles. SARA slaps him lightly on the arm.*)

**LEO.** Okay, what part of this am I *not* supposed to laugh at?

**SARA.** (*re: pills*) Here, take these. (*looks at bottle*) No, don't take these.

(*She sets them on the coffee table.*)

**YURI.** Who is dislocating your arm? The kid or the mother?

(*LEO laughs again. YURI heads off again in search of Tylenol.*)

**SARA.** No, that was at the hospital.

**LEO.** You like hospitals, don't you, pal?

**TOM.** (*increasingly irate*) I don't like hospitals.

**SARA.** It was a nurse. She insisted he ride in a wheelchair. Tom was…is agitated the right word?

**TOM.** I don't like hospitals, okay???

**LEO.** Mini-putting and emergency rooms. Quite the hot date, aren't ya?

**TOM.** Fuck you, Leo!!!

(*Silence. YURI stops dead upon his entrance from the hallway.*)

**SARA.** Okay, stop it.

Both of you.

Dad, you promised to be nicer.

**LEO.** That doesn't sound like something I'd say.

**SARA.** Apologize.

**LEO.** What?

**SARA.** Apologize to each other. Apologize and call a truce.

**LEO.** Truce?

**SARA.** Apologize.

**LEO.** I'm pretty sure I'm doing something else right now.

**SARA.** Dad!

**TOM.** I'll go first.

Leo:

I'm sorry.

I shouldn't have told you to fuck off.

That was wrong.

I'm in considerable pain.

**SARA.** Thank you, Tom.

*(to* **LEO***)* Dad?

(**LEO** *takes a bite of sandwich and indicates his mouth is full of food.*)

**TOM.** Forget it.

**SARA.** No, Dad –

**TOM.** *(starts for the door)* I'm leaving.

**LEO.** Have a nice flight!

**SARA.** Jesus, Daddy, just apologize!!!

**LEO.** Why should I?

**SARA.** BECAUSE I LOVE HIM.

BECAUSE I LOVE HIM, OKAY?

And I don't want you screwing things up again!!!

*(Silence.* **SARA** *knows she's crossed a line she shouldn't have crossed.)*

I'm sorry.

I didn't mean…

**LEO**. Why do you have to spoil it?

Hasn't it been nice for a while? Just the two of us.

What do you need *him* for?

I've always been the one to look after this family.

No one understands protection like I do, that's all I'm trying to do.

To protect you, sweetheart.

From yourself.

You do this. I'm sorry, honey, but you do.

You attract people to you, and they just let you down.

**TOM**. Leo –

**LEO**. PETS!!!

Christ, even the pets are unreliable!

It's not your fault, darling, it's just nothing wants to stick around you for long.

(**SARA** *is in tears.*)

I don't know why.

The world's full of fickle people. Fickle cats. Fickle fish.

I stick around. Huh?

You just don't know any better. You lose a husband, you try to find another. You lose a fish, you buy a dozen more. You're selfish, sweetheart, I'm sorry, but your mother was right, you've always been a selfish little girl.

You can't insure yourself against loss, honey, but you can stop repeating the same stupid mistakes.

**TOM**. You're a bastard, you know that?

**SARA**. Tom, can you please leave. You too, Yuri.

**YURI**. *(stirring the pot on stove)* I still haven't eaten.

**SARA**. Please?

**LEO**. Fine!!!

I'll apologize.

If it'll get everyone off my back!

But for the record, I don't know why I'm doing it. I can't remember the last time I did anything wrong!

*(He clears his throat.)*

LEO. *(cont.)* I.

I'm.

*(He shuffles back and forth on his feet.)*

I'm sss… I'm fffsss…

*(He suddenly turns and exits to bedrooms.)*

*(pause)*

*(The phone rings.)*

(**TOM** *looks over at* **SARA.**)

(**SARA** *picks it up and hands it to* **TOM.**)

TOM. *(into phone)* Hi.

No, it's Tom.

Yes, that Tom.

Okay.

Okay.

Okay.

Thank you.

(**TOM** *hangs up. A moment.)*

*(to* **SARA,** *as he puts his coat on)* I'll call you tomorrow?

*(He starts to leave.* **LEO** *re-enters.)*

LEO. Bread's stale.

(**TOM** *turns back.)*

The bread?

TOM. I just bought it.

LEO. Well…

TOM. You know…you didn't have to eat that.

LEO. You want me to starve?

TOM. I brought left-overs. Every day this week. All you had to do was reheat them.

LEO. Sara doesn't cook.

TOM. Microwave them.

**LEO.** She has EHS.

**TOM.** Then do it yourself. You're not helpless.

**LEO.** I'll be the judge of that!

Where are these so-called leftovers?

**YURI.** *(guiltily)* You said I could eat them.

**SARA.** It's fine, Yuri.

**TOM.** I'll get more bread.

**LEO.** Do you know when? Can you approximate?

**SARA.** Dad.

**TOM.** I got a busy couple weeks here.

**LEO.** Oh, yeah? Is the nation on High Alert, or somethin'?

**TOM.** I've got training in Virginia coming up, that's all.

**LEO.** Sounds important. Is it important?

Some new screening criteria? Further limitations on lotions and unguents? It's a good thing you took that oath, we all feel so much safer with you around.

*(Pause. **TOM** doesn't take the bait.)*

**TOM.** I'll make sure you guys are good before I take off.

**LEO.** Mustard.

**TOM.** Excuse me?

**LEO.** Musss-tttard.

**TOM.** I just got some, Leo.

**LEO.** The wrong kind. I like the kind with the seeds.

And more bread.

Russian rye.

And grab some Tylenol while you're at it. In case of emergencies.

**YURI.** And toilet paper.

*(**TOM** and **SARA** glare at **YURI**.)*

I notice you're getting low.

*(**TOM** crosses angrily towards the door.)*

**LEO.** Better write it down, Scatterbrain!

**TOM.** I don't need to write it down, Leo… *(tapping his head)* it's all right up here: bread, mustard, Tylenol, T.P.!!! Anything else?

*(Pause.* **TOM** *starts to leave.)*

**LEO.** Thanks… *Brad!*

**TOM.** Goddamnit!!!

**LEO.** Oops!
My mistake. You're not Brad.
I forgot.
Brad's dead.

**SARA.** DAD!

**TOM.** What's he talking about?

**SARA.** Just go!

**TOM.** Someone tell me who the hell Brad is?

**SARA.** Dad, go to your room.

**LEO.** What am I, six?

**SARA.** Yeah, sometimes, yes! *(turns on* **YURI***)* Yuri, I'm sorry but what are you doing…???

**YURI.** I haven't eaten today.

**LEO.** I have no idea what she ever saw in him.

**TOM.** You were talking about Brad, right Leo?

**LEO.** That depends. Who are you?

**SARA.** Can't you see you're just confusing him?

**TOM.** The guy who married your daughter?

**LEO.** *(in protest, to* **TOM***)* I never gave you my blessing!!!

**SARA.** Just stop it, Tom! Daddy, Dad listen to me…Dad?

**TOM.** I don't get it, what's the big mystery, Sara?

**LEO.** Oh, it's a doozy!

**SARA.** *(to* **TOM***)* Leave him alone. He doesn't know anything.

**LEO.** Don't underestimate me!

**SARA.** I told you not to ask me questions. We stood in this room, and I *asked* you…didn't I? Can't you respect that?

**TOM.** But if you answered I'd be…

SARA. Be what?

TOM. Better prepared, I guess.

SARA. For what?

TOM. I don't know. For all of it, the weirdness. All of this
weird shit that seems to befall you… So talk.
You had an ex-husband. It happens. I had an ex-wife.

SARA. I know, Tom, I'm well aware. You seem quite proud of
that little tidbit of information.

TOM. I'm not, okay?

SARA. You don't need to know the answer to every little
thing just to go on a lousy date with me.

TOM. Lousy date?

SARA. Yeah, you know, you don't need to worry about it.
Because we're done!

TOM. What are you talking about?

SARA. We're done. I'm done. Get out.

TOM. Okay – you said you were in love with me.

SARA. I changed my mind. I'm fickle.

YURI. I warned you.

TOM. Shut up, Yuri. *(to SARA)* You think a few bumps and
bruises are gonna scare me off?

YURI. Did I tell you about the dog bites?

SARA. Leave. Now!

YURI. Take the chance while you have it.

TOM. No one asked you!

LEO. Wow, this is boring, I'm going to bed.

*(LEO starts to shuffle down the hallway.)*

SARA. *(final, emphatic, to TOM)* Go!!!.

TOM. *(heads LEO off)* Tell me about Brad. Leo? What
happened?

LEO. *(tumbling out uncontrollably)* She should never have
married him, he was bad news, and always with the
money problems…

SARA. Tom, get out of here or…or…damn it, Tom, I swear I'll call the police.

(*She picks up the phone and threatens to dial.*)

LEO. I'm not a religious man. But I used to pray that she'd wakeup from whatever trance she was in, she'd open her eyes and finally see him for what he was, the way the rest of us saw him.

SARA. You were the only one Dad!

LEO. He'd drop by unannounced.

SARA. I invited him over.

LEO. And raid my refrigerator.

SARA. IT'S NOT YOUR GODDAMNED REFRIGERATOR!!!

LEO. Thank god he killed himself!

(SARA *screams out. Madness! The pot that* YURI *has been cooking the leftovers in suddenly catches fire and the smoke alarm goes off.* TOM *goes to grab it and burns his hand severely. He wets a dishtowel and wraps it around his hand.*)

(YURI *is jumping up and down, using another towel to waft the smoke away from the detector, all the while uttering "Likho, Likho." The smoke detector eventually falls silent.*)

(LEO *turns and slowly exits.*)

(TOM *looks across at* SARA. *He takes a step in her direction.*)

SARA. (*throws her hand up*) I can't tell you. I can't say it. Don't ask. Please. I can't. I just can't.

(*A moment, then* TOM *walks out. Several bulbs fizzle out.* YURI *opens the cupboard with the bulbs and starts to go around replacing them.*)

Leave it.

(YURI *leaves as fast as he can.* SARA *sits alone in the darkened room.*)

### Three

*(In the darkness, we hear the sound of a heavy rainstorm.*
*As lights fade up we hear the blip, blip, blip of the leaky*
*roof.* **SARA** *is on the couch. The roof starts to drip right*
*into Frank's fish bowl. She relocates it to the other end of*
*the coffee table but after a few seconds, it starts to drip*
*into the bowl again.* **SARA** *lets out an audible sigh and*
*sits there for a moment pensively watching the fish swim*
*lazily round the bowl.)*

**SARA.** Hi, fish.

Hi, Frank.

Hey, Frankie.

How you doing, buddy?

*(***LEO** *enters.)*

**LEO.** Who you talking to?

**SARA.** Myself.

**LEO.** You hungry?

**SARA.** I'm going for a walk.

**LEO.** It's raining.

**SARA.** Don't wait up, okay?

*(pause)*

**LEO.** Are you mad at me?

**SARA.** The roof's leaking. Be careful where you sit.

*(She starts to put on her coat.)*

**LEO.** What time is it?

**SARA.** *(turns, levels him with this:)* Do you love me?

**LEO.** You're going for a walk?

**SARA.** Dad! Do you?

**LEO.** What kinda question is that?

**SARA.** I just... I can't remember you ever saying, I mean,
actually saying the words 'I love you.'

**LEO.** Don't be ridiculous. Of course I've said it.

**SARA.** When?

    Can you remember when?

    Did you ever say it to mom? Can you say it now?

    *(He is silent.)*

    You got what you wanted, Dad. Like you always do. He's gone. You won.

    *(She starts for the door.)*

**LEO.** I'm trying to protect you!

**SARA.** Like you protected Mom?

**LEO.** Who kept this family together, huh? After she disappeared???

**SARA.** She didn't disappear, Dad. You –

**LEO.** I watched her. With my own two eyes…walk right out that door.

**SARA.** Forget it. *(opening the door)* Go back to bed.

**LEO.** Where are you going? Sara?

**SARA.** Maybe I'll disappear, too.

    *(She leaves. The door slams shut.)*

**LEO.** Sara! Sara!!!

    *(**LEO** just stands there, a look of panic on his face, as the lights fade and sound cross-fades into the next scene.)*

## Four

*(Outside, the rain is still coming down. In the darkness, we hear the phone ringing. Lights fade up on an empty stage. After a moment,* **LEO** *shuffles on from the bedroom hallway in his pajamas and slippers, a portable phone in hand.)*

**LEO.** Sara?

*(Hearing no response,* **LEO** *dials the number again. A beat, and then the phone starts to ring on stage again. There is obviously no answer.* **LEO** *hangs up.)*

*(Now disoriented and growing agitated, he shuffles over to the couch and sits. He sets the receiver down and finds the bottle of pills on the coffee table. He rattles the pills inside the bottle.)*

**LEO.** Sara?

Two in the morning, two at night.

*(He opens the bottle and dispenses a couple into the palm of his hand. The instant he swallows them, he seems suddenly surprised by the bottle still in his hands...so he dispenses a couple more.)*

**LEO.** Two in the morning, two at night.

*(Reaching out to set down the pills, he now locates the fish bowl with Frank swimming around inside. He pulls it toward him, sloshing some water over the lip. For a second, it almost looks like* **LEO** *is watching the fish – but he's sensing it – staring blankly out for quite some time, then...)*

*(He reaches into the bowl, grabs the fish and pulls it out of the water. It gently flips around on the palm of his hand. A beat.)*

*(***LEO** *suddenly, and quite unexpectedly, puts the fish in his mouth, closes his eyes and swallows it whole. He sits for a moment, seemingly unaware of what he's done...*

*then it dawns on him. He panics. He gags. He coughs
and tries to regurgitate the fish, but he cannot. He starts
to cry out...)*

*(He now reaches for the phone to call Sara again,
accidentally scattering pills across the coffee table to the
floor. He gathers them up...three, four, a dozen, more...
into the palm of his hand.)*

LEO. *(under his breath)* Two in the morning, two at night.

*(He swallows the lot. He tries to crunch them up but
there's too many, so he grabs the fish bowl and takes a
large swallow of water.)*

*(A moment here, and then the front door opens and
SARA comes in, her arms full of grocery bags. The light
in the hallway is out again. It's dark and she blindly
makes her way into the kitchen area.)*

LEO. Dad, I'm home.

*(LEO just sits there, motionless, as SARA unpacks one or
two items and then heads down the hallway.)*

SARA. *(off)* Dad?

*(After a second, she returns to the living room. She tries
the light switch. One of the bulbs goes on for a second
and then pops out. She crosses to the kitchen. She goes to
switch on the lights, but the bulbs are all out. She opens
the refrigerator door and the light streams into the living
room where she finally sees her father.)*

SARA. Daddy? What are you doing?

LEO. Estelle?

SARA. It's me, Dad; it's Sara.

LEO. Sara.

SARA. Dad, what's wrong?

LEO. I think...I think I've done something bad.

SARA. *(going to him)* What is it?

LEO. I think your mother left us because I...

**SARA.** It's okay.

**LEO.** What did I do? Sara? What did I do?

**SARA.** You didn't do anything, Dad.

**LEO.** Then why won't she come back?

I did something terrible.

Didn't I?

Tell me. I can't remember.

What did I do?

**SARA.** It was just a bad dream.

It's okay.

*(She holds her father's head in her lap. She strokes his hair. But then she sees the empty pill bottle. She grabs it.)*

Dad?????

*(blackout)*

### Five

*(SARA, alone. We think she's talking to herself, curled up on the couch with her head pressed against her hand, but in a moment she will reposition herself and reveal she's actually talking to someone on the phone. This is difficult.)*

**SARA.** Dad was crazy about fireworks.

Every year we'd go up to the roof to ring in the New Year.

Fourth of July, New Year's Eve, hands-down his favorite holidays.

So: up we'd go. No matter the weather.

At midnight, Mom would start banging pots and pans like a lunatic, and Dad would lead us all in a tuneless rendition of "Auld Lang Syne" as we watched the Denver skyline light up.

I was nineteen when I met Brad.

Dad hated him. From the second he met him, he never gave Brad a chance. And he was a good guy, he really was.

We got married, without my father's blessing, which I know sounds so totally nineteenth century, but I think maybe I did it to piss my dad off. And it worked.

Anyway…Brad started having money problems, and I convinced Dad to help him out, or rather my mother did. It was supposed to be a temporary thing. Helping out at the office. But Dad liked to do everything himself, never trusted anyone, was always so… *meticulous.*

We don't know how it happened, okay, because Brad would be doing paperwork? And Dad would be over his shoulder, *watching* his every move, making him retype forms, two and three times, and…*somehow…* Dad forgot, or maybe Brad, I don't know…but they didn't file Mom's insurance properly, didn't check the right box, didn't file within the specified time, some dumb little thing... and we had no idea she wasn't covered when she got sick.

For eight months she suffered.

There *were* specialists... there *were* places we could have taken her...but the bills kept piling up...and Mom refused to let Dad sell the business. Refused. *(beat)* We lost it anyway. And then we lost Mom. And Dad ...

He would sit home all day by the phone, with his briefcase, taking calls from imaginary clients like nothing had ever happened to the one client he should have... He kept showing up at the office, even after the new owners moved in. The cops had to tear him away from what was once his desk, screaming, "It's not your office, this is my office!"

And everything was Brad's fault.

It was New Year's Eve...the first since Mom died. And we're up there just like old times, Dad and Brad, and I've taken over the pots and pans duty for Mom and I'm banging away because it's midnight and it's what I do now, every year. I'm banging my little heart out when I hear Brad scream. I turn around and he's gone. Vanished. Somehow slipped and fallen from the roof.

Dad woke up the next morning.

He couldn't remember what happened on that roof.

And he couldn't see a thing.

*(The front door swings open.* **TOM** *is standing there, his cellphone to his ear.* **SARA** *doesn't notice him at first.)*

That was twenty-two years ago.
And I've had a problem with light bulbs ever since.
Are you still there?

*(***TOM*** *drifts into the room.)*

**TOM.** *(still on the phone)* Was Brad the only one?

**SARA.** *(turning to him, still on the phone herself)* There's been a couple others.

**TOM.** I mean, who…

Did they all die?

**SARA.** There's been a lot of nosebleeds. One guy lost the sensation in his toes.

**TOM.** Just his toes?

**SARA.** Uhuh.

**TOM.** Okay, good.

**SARA.** Another guy just got speeding tickets whenever we went out. Like *every* time.

**TOM.** That's kinda funny, actually.

**SARA.** He couldn't afford to go out with me, his insurance was so high.

**TOM.** Yuri thinks you cursed him.

**SARA.** I lost his mother's cat.

**TOM.** He almost broke his neck.

And the whole ladder incident?

**SARA.** Oh, yeah.

Are you going to leave now?

**TOM.** It is kinda late.

**SARA.** I mean…*leave*-leave.

**TOM.** Can I think about it?

**SARA.** Uhuh.

> *(silence as* **TOM** *thinks about it)*

**TOM.** I don't think so.

**SARA.** Are you sure?

> *(He thinks about it some more.)*

**TOM.** Uhuh.

**SARA.** Something might happen to you.

**TOM.** Something already has.

**SARA.** I'm worried you'll get hurt. Aren't you worried?

**TOM.** I'm a little worried.

SARA. You're not afraid?

TOM. I work for Homeland Security.

SARA. My dad worked in insurance.

TOM. He didn't have a badge.

SARA. I'm gonna hang up now.

TOM. Okay.

(*She hangs up.* TOM *still has his phone pressed to his ear.*)

SARA. You should hang up too.

(*They both hang up. They stand there.*)

TOM. How is he?

SARA. He's going to be fine.

Thanks for getting him to the hospital so fast that night.

I know you don't like hospitals.

TOM. I can't stop looking at you.

SARA. I know. It's weird.

TOM. *You're* weird.

And your dad's weird.

You're both *really* weird.

And I can't stop looking at you.

(*a beat*)

How's the foot?

SARA. Better. Bit achey.

How was Virginia?

TOM. Virginia was…devoid of you.

Do you think…?

SARA. Uhuh?

TOM. You might be up for some dancing?

I wanna take you dancing.

SARA. Seriously?

TOM. I have these moves. You've never seen my moves.

*(A beat. **TOM** tilts his head to one side, trying to wrap his head around this next thing.)*

Your dad ate your fish?

*(**SARA** nods. **TOM** takes a twenty dollar bill out of his wallet.)*

**SARA**. What's this?

**TOM**. *(hands it to her)* A bet's a bet.

You know what I think? I think it's over. I think whatever it is, whatever's been plaguing you all these years, this *fucking weirdness*...I think it's over and done with, I do...it's run its course. By telling me, you know, just now, by having the courage to say *that thing* you've been so scared to say, I think you've overcome it...it's been exorcised.

**SARA**. Yeah?

**TOM**. Yeah.

*(A hockey puck crashes through the window. **SARA** doesn't react. **TOM**, well, he just tries to stay in the moment.)*

**TOM**. Will you marry me?

**SARA**. No.

**TOM**. Take your time.

*(quick beat)*

**SARA**. No.

**TOM**. Okay.

*(He starts to leave.)*

**SARA**. Not without my father's blessing.

*(**TOM** turns to her; he exhales audibly. Blackout.)*

## Six

*(Late afternoon, July 4th.* **TOM** *and* **LEO** *are sitting at opposite ends of the couch.* **TOM** *is holding a little American flag, staring intently at* **LEO**. **LEO** *is dunking one of his favorite cookies in his coffee and staring off into space. An uncomfortably long silence.)*

**TOM**. Aren't you going to say something?

**LEO**. Can you give me an example?

**TOM**. I just asked for your daughter's hand in marriage.

*(beat)*

I assumed you'd have some kind of reaction.

*(***LEO*** *stands. He calmly pours the contents of his coffee cup into* **TOM***'s lap. He hands* **TOM** *the empty cup, walks across the room and overturns a side table, sending all of its contents crashing to the floor. He then uses his cane to knock several books off a bookshelf. Finally, there is a decorative ornament on one of the shelves which he delicately picks up and casually drops onto the floor where it shatters. He sits back down.)*

*(brief pause)* So, is that a 'No?'

**LEO**. I've been holding that in for a long time.

*(beat)*

**TOM**. These khakis are brand new, you know?

**LEO**. Where is Sara?

**TOM**. *(mopping up his crotch with a napkin)* Getting buns for the burgers. They're my nice khakis.

**LEO**. Does she know about this scheme of yours?

**TOM**. No, I just decided to ask you for her hand in marriage and not say anything to her because it's, you know, July 4th, 1776 *not* 2014, so…

**LEO**. Do you really think this is the time to be cute with me?

*(pause)*

**TOM**. I would like an answer.

   If possible.

   By the end of the day.

**LEO**. And if I refuse to give my blessing? How will the whole
   scenario play out?

**TOM**. Sara would prefer –

**LEO**. Answer the question.

**TOM**. No. I don't think she'd go through with it. It's that
   important to her.

   *(beat)*

**LEO**. Did you buy these cookies?

**TOM**. *(tentatively)* Maybe.

**LEO**. So it's a bribe.

**TOM**. It's a cookie.

**LEO**. But you got the wrong kind, so it's a really bad bribe.

**TOM**. These are *exactly* the same kind, I took the empty
   packet to the store so I wouldn't get the wr...

**LEO**. Are you calling me a liar? I have an acute sense of
   taste. Didn't we go over this?

**TOM**. Yeah, I know, and *smell*...and *hearing*. It's been
   established. *(re: his pants)* This is uncomfortable.

**LEO**. You can say that again.

**TOM**. I think I'm gonna go change.

   *(He starts for the door.)*

**LEO**. She did it before.

   Got married without my blessing.

   *(a beat)*

   You don't have to say anything.

   *(**TOM** wasn't.)*

   You don't have to gloat. *(**TOM** isn't.)* I was obviously
   wrong about certain things. I was confused. Apparently.
   Concerning your...identity.

   *(brief pause)*

   But I *was*.

**TOM.** What?

**LEO.** Fucking with you. Sometimes. When I called you Brad.

**TOM.** Okay.

**LEO.** But other times…

*(He just shakes his head, sadly.)*

I don't have anything further to say.

*(**TOM** moves toward the door again.)*

I lost my wife. I don't know if you know that.

I wake up sometimes and I can suddenly see.

I wander round the apartment…looking at everything, like, for the first time.

Wallpaper, dust.

Colors.

How the light comes in the windows.

I sometimes think I'm going to see her.

But then I wake up *again* and realize…

*(He sighs.)*

But that doesn't mean that I automatically, by default, suddenly like you, okay, because in fact I don't particularly like anyone, so…put that in your pipe and smoke it.

**TOM.** Are you trying to say you're sorry?

**LEO.** Don't ever quote me.

*(a beat)*

Go change your pants. You look like you wet yourself.

**TOM.** How do you…? *(Meaning: "Know what it looks like?")*

**LEO.** Well, doesn't it?

*(It does. And there's a moment here where we might just wonder if **LEO** has actually regained his sight.)*

**TOM.** *(starts to leave, then…)* I'm gonna take care of her.

**LEO.** Don't make promises you can't keep.

**TOM.** I will, though, I'll protect her.

**LEO**. Didn't they teach you anything at Homeland Security? There is no protection. Against even those things with the lowest probability. If probability is not absolutely zero, then it can and will happen. Tragedy. Failure. Accident. Loss.

(**TOM** *turns back from the doorway. Pause. He's never said this before.*)

**TOM**. I was married.

She died.

We got divorced. And *then* she died.

In case you're wondering about the chronology there.

At the funeral…

I felt this pressure to say something. Something meaningful. Or just not totally meaning*less*. But when I stood up in front of everyone, all that came out was, "Lila taught me how to Salsa." It was true, but… I'm sure most people assumed I'd left her when she started getting sick, right? That I'd up and quit when the going got tough, but that's not…

I stayed with her.

I hate hospitals.

(*A beat, then…*)

(*We hear a toilet flush and* **YURI** *enters from the hallway.*)

(**TOM** *looks at* **YURI**, *surprised.* **YURI** *looks at* **TOM**, *not surprised.*)

Hey.

**YURI**. Hey.

(*A beat.* **TOM** *turns to* **LEO**.)

**TOM**. Can I marry your daughter?

(**YURI** *looks at* **LEO**. *Pause.*)

**LEO**. I got three things to say:

(**SARA** *comes through the front door with a King Sooper's grocery bag filled with hamburger buns, etc.*)

**SARA.** I got buns!

**LEO.** D'you get fireworks?

**SARA.** City banned 'em. It was on the radio.

**LEO.** They're trying to ruin my Fourth of July.

**SARA.** It's not *your* Fourth of July, dad. It's the wildfires.
They're worried. But they're still doing 'em up at Mile
High, so…chop-chop.

*(She suddenly notices the carnage left by **LEO**.)*

What happened here?

**LEO.** I had a reaction.

**SARA.** *(re: **TOM**'s pants)* What happened to you?

**LEO.** He wet himself.

**TOM.** *(heading out)* I'll be right back.

**SARA.** Hurry, you're the grill man!
Yuri? Are you, uh…? *(Meaning: "staying?")*

**YURI.** I'm invited?

**SARA.** Are you hungry?

**YURI.** Haven't eaten all day.

**LEO.** What is it with you?

**SARA.** Can you take this stuff up? And help dad.

**LEO.** I don't need help.

**SARA.** Just…fine.

*(**SARA** hands **LEO** the phone.)*

Here. In case of emergencies.

*(**LEO** looks at her a moment – is he going to say
something? – but he just takes the phone and gives it
a little shake in acknowledgment. He and **YURI** leave.
**SARA** goes to the kitchen to grab condiments, etc.)*

*(**TOM** suddenly appears again in the doorway. He
has **SARA**'s itinerant cat in his arms\*. He stops on the
threshold noticing that for the first time in the play the
bulb in the hallway outside the door is working.)*

---

\*See Appendix for alternate dialogue.

**TOM.** Hey, the light's working. Is this your cat?

**SARA.** Oh my god!!!

**TOM.** She was just sitting at the bottom of the stairs. What's her name? She's cute.

**SARA.** He.

**TOM.** What's his name?

**SARA.** Cat.

**TOM.** Hello, Cat. I'm Tom.

*(He hands Cat to **SARA**.)*

**SARA.** Hey, there, stranger.

Come on we're going to miss the fireworks.

*(She runs toward the door with Cat in her arms.)*

**TOM.** Aren't you forgetting something?

*(**TOM** goes to the kitchen and grabs the pots and pans.)*

**SARA.** Those are New Year's, not the Fourth.

**TOM.** I'm starting a new tradition.

*(**TOM**'s phone rings.)*

This better not be work! I been covering shifts all month for this.

*(into phone)* Hello? Yeah, it's Tom. Leo?

*(He looks at **SARA**.)*

Okay.

*(Quick little beat.)*

Okay.

*(Little longer beat. He smiles at **SARA**.)*

And what's the third thing?

*(And just one more beat. He hangs up, and looks at **SARA**.)*

I should really be in uniform for this.

*(He takes **SARA**'s hand, and slowly drops to his knee.)*

I, do solemnly swear, that I will protect and defend
you against all enemies, foreign and domestic; against
all harm, bad luck or hockey pucks; that I will bear
true faith and allegiance to the same; that I take this
obligation freely, without any mental reservation or
purpose of evasion; and that I will well and faithfully
discharge the duties of the office on which I am about
to enter. So help me God.

*(They kiss.)*

*(Fade in the sound of fireworks exploding in the sky
above the apartment building, as the lights slowly fade
to black.)*

**End of Play**

# APPENDIX

It's my preference that all productions use a live cat; however, I'm a realist, and recognize the unpredictability of this choice. About a week before we opened at Riverside Theatre, we decided to cut the cat. As Leo would say, he was too "unreliable." Feline Equity was notified. So I came up with an offstage solution, as follows:

(**TOM** *suddenly appears again in the doorway. He has* **SARA**'s *itinerant cat in his arms. He stops on the threshold noticing that for the first time in the play the bulb in the hallway outside the door is working.*)

**TOM.** Hey, the light's working. (*From the doorway, he points off down the hallway stairs.*) Is this your cat?

**SARA.** (*crosses to the doorway, looks off*) Oh my god!!!

**TOM.** She was just sitting at the bottom of the stairs.

(*They head into the hallway, out of sight momentarily. From off …*)

(*off*) What's her name? She's cute.

**SARA.** (*off*) He.

**TOM.** (*off*) What's his name?

**SARA.** (*off*) Cat.

**TOM.** (*off*) Hello, Cat. I'm Tom.

**SARA.** (*off*) Hey, there, stranger.

(*A pause, and then… They both react.*)

**TOM.** (*off*) Oop! There he goes.

**SARA.** (*off*) Awww, oh well.

**TOM.** (*off*) Send a postcard!

(*They return to the stage.*)

**SARA.** Come on, we're going to miss the fireworks.

(*She runs toward the door.*)

[return to text]

# PRODUCTION NOTES

*Sara's problem with light bulbs:*
Beginning in Scene One and continuing throughout the play, the light bulbs in Sara's apartment are constantly popping, fizzling, flickering, burning out and generally not functioning reliably. These moments are obviously very easily handled with light cues – however, I have found them to be even more effective (and funnier, as it turns out) if accompanied by sound cues to reinforce the idea there's something terribly wrong with Sara's electrical system.

*Sara's glasses that shatter all the time:*
While there are references in the play to Sara's glasses shattering "all the time," it actually only happens twice in the play: once in the opening scene (Tom clinks glasses with Sara and Sara's shatters) and once right at the end of the first act, as a button, a little claptrap (Tom and Sara clink glasses, and Tom's shatters.) The one at the end of the act is, of course, easier to deal with, because you can use the interval between the acts to clean up the mess. The first instance is a little trickier: you must rely on the actors in the unfolding scene to clean up the spillage of liquid while continuing the dialogue.

Productions have addressed the issue of breaking glasses on stage in a variety of ways: some producers chose to invest in the expense of breakable glasses and save the time and energy one might invest in more affordable solutions. Breakable glassware specifically manufactured for stage and film use is not cheap, however, and even though you only break a couple of glasses per night, (depending on the length of your run) it does add up. Alternatively, there are also pre-fab molds that can be purchased in order to fabricate your own breakable glassware – however, theatres that elected to go this route reported that quality control was sometimes an issue, and that it can be quite time-consuming.

The technical team at Riverside Theatre came up with what I believe to be the best solution: they purchased very low-cost plastic wine glasses (Yay, Dollar Store) and then scored them in such a fashion that they shattered exactly where they wanted them to break, almost without fail. While plastic glasses don't make the same sound as real glass when it breaks (although, sugar glasses don't sound particularly realistic either!) it has been my experience that the moment in the play happens so fast, that, combined with Tom's reaction to the shattering glass in his hand, the audience is completely fooled. After all, it's quite a shock for them also to see a glass break on stage – it usually only happens accidentally. So, once again, the simple magic of the theatre wins the day!

### Sara's leaky roof:
This is probably the technical effect that's most daunting to producers. How to make the roof leak? is one thing. But…how to the make the roof leak move is quite another. It might alleviate concerns to know that the audience does "perceive" quite a bit of leakiness with only a little bit of effort. It helps that there are pots and pans scattered widely about the apartment in order to catch the drips from previous rainy and snowy days, so in a way we've already set them up for it.

The roof physically leaks in only two scenes in the play – during the 'pre-date' scene with Sara and Tom – and it's described as an intermittent 'blip-blip-blip' from the leaky roof – so much of the effect can be achieved simply with atmospheric sound effects, and perhaps a single drip into a single bucket, etc. The second instance is the trickier one to pull off, but I think it's well-worth figuring it out because the moment is an important story point in the arc of the central protagonist. It is the moment when Sara's fears have come true and the roof has started to drip right into the fish bowl. She relocates the fish bowl to the other end of the coffee table, and it starts to drip into the bowl once again. At a bare minimum you can probably get away with having just two or three spots onstage for the leaks to come from.

Once again, different productions have solved this moment with varying degrees of success, and with varying investments of resources. Some theatres rigged their lighting grids with hoses and tubing with strategically placed holes/valves/spigots, etc. to control the rate of flow, allowing someone backstage to turn things on and off. Turning the drips on was the easy thing; shutting the drips off often proved more difficult. The occasional unwanted drip has been the feature of a couple productions that come to mind. These "high-tech" solutions were successful by and large, but required a goodly amount of time to rehearse the drips to get it down to a science. Other theatres used very simple solutions – everything from hanging two-liter soda bottles in levered rigs with duct tape over the mouth that could be upended to start the drips and then turned back to stop the flow of water. Simple, simple. The technical director at Riverside Theatre designed a simple but wonderfully effective drip rig, and a mechanical sketch is provided below. (A full set of mechanical drawings can be obtained from Riverside Theatre by contacting

Technical Director Violet Virnig: technical@riversidetheatre. org.) The below image is reprinted by permission.

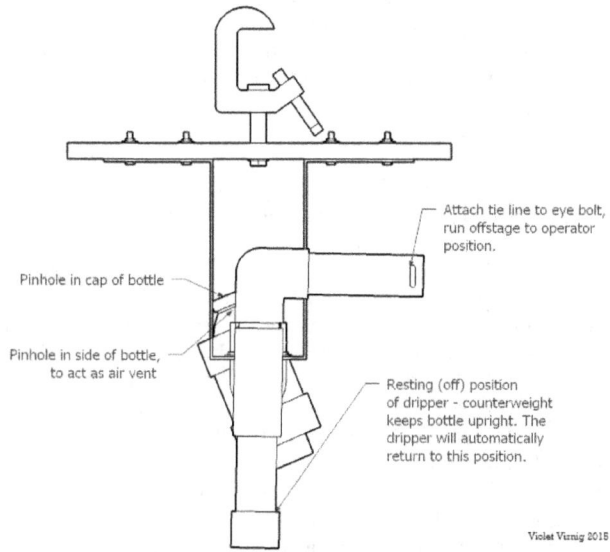

Attach tie line to eye bolt, run offstage to operator position.

Pinhole in cap of bottle

Pinhole in side of bottle, to act as air vent

Resting (off) position of dripper - counterweight keeps bottle upright. The dripper will automatically return to this position.

Violet Virnig 2015

***CRASH!!!! A hockey puck smashes through the apartment window:***
This is an effect that is actually much simpler to achieve than you might think. One production actually installed sugar glass windows that shattered every night as the puck hurtled through the window. It sounded great, but it was bitch to clean up, and made for longer scene transitions. Plus, if any of the sugar glass remained on stage, actors would invariably step on it in subsequent crunchy scenes. And, truth-be-told, the puck comes through the window so quickly (and the audience isn't expecting it to happen) so it actually doesn't register with the eye until after the puck is on stage and the window broken. So...once again, I suggest you keep it simple.

When I wrote the scene, I never even imagined there would be glass of any kind in the window frame. I was channeling some school play or other I was in as a kid, some farce, in which a window was broken in the play by a maniacal paper boy. In that production our resourceful stage manager was responsible backstage for chucking the paper through the window. The "window" was non-existent, because our resourceful set designer had simply hung drapes, which billowed wonderfully when the stage manager chucked the paper through them, aided and abetted by our resourceful sound designer who added the cue of glass breaking. And, hey presto! Problem solved. The lamp that gets knocked over in my scene is optional – I thought it was a funny coda to the mayhem of the puck crashing through the window. Dare I suggest rigging it with good old-fashioned fishing line, and the "practical" snaps out when it falls?

### Yuri and the leftovers:

In the climactic scene of the play (Act Two, Scene Two) at the moment when Leo reveals what happened to Sara's husband, the pot in which Yuri is reheating the leftovers catches fire. The text suggests that it's a pan on the stovetop that catches fire, but a very simple and helpful solution was imagined by the design team at New Jersey Repertory Company. Instead of placing the leftovers in a pot on top of the stove, Yuri there placed the leftovers inside the oven – this simple change allowed the technical director to rig up a smoke machine, and the closed oven door contained the smoke until the moment the smoke detector goes off and Tom opened up the oven, causing the trapped smoke to billow out in dramatic fashion. Lovely! The chaos then of Tom's hand getting burned, and Yuri's attempt to waft away the smoke from the ear-piercing smoke detector, created exactly the effect I wished to achieve without having to mess with any pyrotechnics.

### Sara's fish:

Of all the technical elements in the play, I think this is the trickiest, because the rather alarming moment in the second act when a disoriented Leo eats Frankie the Fish, is predicated on the audience having seen a convincingly live fish at other points in the play. Again, I have learned a variety of lessons from the ways in which different technical teams tackled this issue – of which there are a couple of interrelated issues:

1. There are fish that have died in the play (Act One, Scene Two) and we watch as Sara scoops them out of the tank.

2. There are "live" fish in the play (ex. when Tom first arrives with a goldfish in a plastic bag as a gift for Sara, or during the date scene when they watch Frankie swimming lazily around the fish bowl) – some theatres have elected to keep a tank of goldfish backstage during the run of the production and use these fish in the couple of instances in which they appear on stage, switching them out with fake fish between scenes in which the focus is not squarely on Frankie. Other theatres used little mechanical fish that scooted around the tank incessantly. Still others used fish that floated and shimmered

but did not exactly swim. I think live fish are the very best solution, but I certainly understand practical or even ethical concerns about having to keep a bunch of goldfish alive backstage during the run of the play. Anyone who's ever won a goldfish for their kid at the county fair knows the vagaries of caretaking and the relatively unpredictable life expectancy of Carassius auratus, the common goldfish.

3. There is a fish onstage that only moments before appears to be alive and then it appears that Leo has eaten it – this is the trickiest moment of the play, where slight-of-hand is required. I was aware that a little bait-and-switch (pardon the pun) needed to take place here, which is why both of these scenes (Act Two, Scene Three and Act Two, Scene Four) take place at night and in relative darkness. The live Frankie gets switched with the edible Frankie in the transition between these scenes.

### Sara's cat:
What can I say? I'm sorry. I broke one of the cardinal rules of the theatre – I put a cat on stage. And I would say, "Cut the cat, don't worry about it," … if it weren't for the fact that the final moments of the play – at those theatres brave enough to figure out how to use a live cat – were simply magical, and helps the play to really come full-circle thematically. I have sensibly limited the amount of stage time the cat gets, chose not to overburden the cat with a tricky monologue, and contained the cat in the very last moments of the play, but I also recognize the burden I have imposed on producers of an already tricky little play. Hence, the safety net of the alternate dialogue (see Appendix.)

The director of the play at Oregon Contemporary Theatre had a theory that certain breeds of cat had better stage presence than others – while I do not fully believe his assertion, I do have to say the cat in his production was marvelous, and behaved better than other felines I have seen cast in the role of Sara's kitty. I believe he adopted the cat in question after the play closed – you may wish to contact him to see if he/she's available (the cat, that is.)

-Robert Caisley
July 2015